The Art of Falling in Love with the Movie Star

SWEETKISS CREEK SERIES

ANNE KEMP

Glen, this one's for us.
xo

ONE

Spencer

If there was ever a day when I needed a pep talk, it's today. Too bad the person on the phone isn't the merriest person to talk to during my existential crisis.

"Spencer, I really wish you'd just stay here in Los Angeles. Why do you have to go back to Sweetkiss Creek so soon?" My father's voice reverberates in the car around me. "You get how lucky you are, right? It's amazing your career gained momentum again since you 'stepped away' from acting for a time-out."

I sit quietly, hoping he'll lose steam, but he doesn't. As usual, he's dusting off his "Daddy knows" soapbox as he steps onto it. I swear, he lives for these moments.

"I had a feeling this was going to happen, that you'd get divided between the thing you want to do and the thing you thought you're supposed to do." His tone tells me he's most likely rolling his eyes at the other end. "I told you that you two shouldn't get married when you did."

This again. "Amelia isn't and wasn't something that I'm 'supposed to do.' I wanted to marry her." Slowing down, I pump the brakes lightly as I approach the main intersection in the center of Sweetkiss Creek. It was snowing earlier when my flight landed, and as if that wasn't enough, the weather gods have decided it's cold enough now for black ice, so I'm not taking any chances.

"You can say what you want, but you know as well as I do that Stoll men aren't supposed to be tied down. We're better off on our own...solo bears in the wild. Mountain men, of sorts. Running free." He stops talking for a brief moment, a sigh slamming against my ear. "Oh, man. I've had another video banned on TikTok for violating community guidelines. What am I doing wrong?"

Never mind the TikTok obsession, his words of advice are laughable coming from a man who recently ended his fourth marriage. Hearing him say the words "Stoll men aren't supposed to be married" makes my stomach anxiously dip. Amelia and the impending failure of our marriage is not a topic we need to talk about right now, so I do what anyone in my shoes would do...ignore him.

"I'm sure you can get the ban overturned. What did you post?"

"I was sharing a video about David McCallum, you know, the guy who played Ducky on *NCIS*, the TV show? You did a guest spot there a few years back."

"I know who you mean. How can you get into trouble posting about him?"

"No clue. I did a side-by-side, that thing where I film myself watching a video of someone else and then I react to it —this one was about Ducky's music career. Did you know some of his music was sampled by Dr. Dre and Snoopy Dog?"

Ladies and gentlemen, my father and my manager. "You did what's called a Duet, Dad, and the name you want to say is Snoop Dogg, not Snoopy. Two different things altogether." Shaking my head, I bite my lip so I don't laugh in his ear. The stoplight before me flicks from green to yellow, and I ease the car into first gear with only some light sliding on the ice before the tires grip and do their thing as it flashes red. "So, are you staying in LA for Christmas this year or are you jet-setting off somewhere tropical?"

To be honest, I don't really care where he's going to be for Christmas, as long as he doesn't show up and try to spend it in Sweetkiss Creek. Being married to Amelia has helped me keep him at bay for several years, but now, without my wife as a shield, I may have to do what I don't want to: tell him no if he says he wants to come. I can always suck it up like a good son would, but there's way too much baggage here for that.

"I'm thinking I'll go to Florida. Key West has a bit of an appeal for me this year...did I tell you about the boat captain I met? She's a looker, Spencer, legs for days and she's quite bossy."

The stoplight flashes bright green, and putting the car into drive, I make my way slowly out of town, heading out into the more rural countryside of Sweetkiss Creek while I listen to him ramble about the latest sweetheart he's met. As I pick up momentum, albeit at a safe speed considering the weather, I'm grateful I'm almost home. Not that I'm headed home, per se, but to the tiny bed-and-breakfast on the outskirts of town where I've been staying since Amelia and I decided to try a trial separation on for size last year.

Let's face it. A bed-and-breakfast is a nice place to be, but it's not my place. It's not home. I'm not even sure where home is anymore, not without Amelia.

But, what I do know is that I need to get off this call with my dad before he goes into more oversharing that I don't want nor do I need to hear. My ears can't take it.

"I'm sure she's a looker, Pops, that is totally your style, but hey..." I tap the steering wheel and look around, taking in the Christmas lights twinkling on a row of brick townhomes on my right and the staged scene of Santa and his reindeer in the front yard to my left. "I'm almost at the inn so I'm gonna let you go. Talk later?"

"I guess." Disappointment drips from his words, but I just can't. I've been hearing that tone since I was little and I don't need to deal with his heaviness, and *his* issues, tonight. I've got my own. "Can you at least let me know if you want to sign the contract for the action film you've been offered? They want to know in the next few days so they can get other roles filled...it's all dependent on you."

"Is that the rom-com action film or the action film with spy elements?" Not that it should really matter, work is work in this business, but I do actually care about where my career is headed these days. "If it's a romantic comedy meets action film, count me in. I want the next project to be fun."

"But the one with spy elements pays more." The manager's tone creeps into my father's voice now. My dad had taken a swing at acting years ago and had some marginal success. He'd done commercials and worked his way up into television. But, at some point, the work had slowed down and, like all things in Hollywood, the shine on his star wore off and he stopped getting work. "I can probably negotiate for more money on the back end or for higher residuals if you do the spy elements —I know one of the executive producers from when I was acting. Sometimes it's about who you know."

I love my dad, but sometimes I get an inkling he likes money more than he likes me. "I appreciate it, but I need fun. Go with fun."

My unspoken thought: I'm going to need to laugh, especially if I end up going through a divorce.

I know. Contradictory to what one would think...in the midst of a love crisis and I'm considering taking the starring role in a romantic comedy? Could be my guilt, but I'll deal with that later. In therapy probably, something my dad should have done after Mom left him.

He clears his throat, seemingly unimpressed. "I'll let you think about it, okay?"

I want to tell him there's no thinking to do, but he won't hear me. A sound like fabric rubbing against his mouthpiece tells me he's more than likely fumbling with his phone. The staticky sound lasts for a few moments before he's back, his voice loud and clear. "Son, I've got another call coming through. Let me know your answer later this week, got it? Talk soon."

With one swift click, he's gone, leaving me still sitting at another intersection waiting for the light to turn green.

I'm busy staring into space, dissecting my father's personality traits and filing them away for future therapy sessions, when I get a twitchy feeling. It's the kind of weird creepiness you get when you *know* someone is watching you—but you're all alone, so how can that be?

Popping my head to the right, I look over and find a car beside mine, but in the turning lane at the intersection. It's an old beat-up Honda Civic with four girls dancing inside it—probably teenagers, but I'm not really sure—and three of them are busy singing their hearts out. One in the backseat is staring at me through her window, her breath hitting the glass with such heat that it fogs instantly. I pull my eyes away quickly, but not before I see her mouth moving and her hand waving excitedly as she wipes the window with a mitten, probably telling the driver to stop, which the driver has done.

I feel like an old man, but kids these days! Stopping in a turn lane. I wish I knew who their parents were; I'd call them up and tell on them. I am, however, prepared for moments like this, and I'm fully aware of what comes next.

First, it's the screams—believe it or not, but you *can* hear four teen girls when they start screaming your name in the car next to you. This is the part of acting I'll never get used to: the part where people recognize me and know me. Or they think they know me because they've read all about me online or in some random magazine.

Next, it's the waving, which is also complemented by the driver yelling at her friends to stop screaming so she can concentrate. The light changes color, and I pull away but keep an eye on my rearview mirror. As I suspected, they pull out behind me and follow me as I drive through the intersection. If I was in LA, I might be more worried than I am now —'cause right now, I'm only thinking that these kids probably need to be at home helping their parents wrap presents or something. They shouldn't be out here on these roads—especially dangerous icy roads at that—and following me.

I'm only a few miles from the inn, but surprisingly, the carload won't get off my tail. Sighing, I turn at the next intersection and aim my car back toward the center of town. Maybe if I pull up outside the Sweetkiss Creek police station, they'll get the hint.

Within minutes, I'm pulling up outside the building that houses Sweetkiss Creek's finest men in blue, slowing my car down so I can slide into a spot right out front. Not thinking, out of force of habit really, I grab my phone to text Amelia and let her know I'm running late. Only realizing before I hit send she doesn't need to know because she's not waiting for me. Not this time.

I take a moment to delete the message, keeping an eye in my rearview on the girls' car. I spot the green paint and see they've parked about half a block away. Close enough to keep tabs on me but, I'm sure in their minds, they think they're hidden in plain sight.

I reach for the phone again, this time to text Sergeant Lane. Typing a quick message, I hit send while keeping an eye on the car behind me. When we first moved here, Amelia insisted we introduce ourselves to the local police and get numbers "just in case" we had a rogue fan show up or something just as creepy. She's a pro; she's handled stuff like this before over the years and knows it comes with the territory, so she's got contingency plans for all the things. I used to give her grief about overthinking and being too prepared, but I take it all back. This is one of those times I'm really glad I listened to her, but it reminds me of how much I miss her, too.

How could we have gotten here? Divorce. D-I-V-O-R-C-E. One word, seven letters in total, but when said aloud I feel like it's a four-letter word I'm dealing with. The D-word, as we used to call it, when we were determined to be together forever.

Beside me, on the passenger seat, sits a stack of papers. Mostly scripts my agent wants me to read while I'm on my self-imposed holiday break, but there's a lone white envelope that has been making its presence known since it arrived last week. Every time I look at it, a cold shiver makes its way down my spine.

A rap on my passenger-side window jolts me from my inner monologue. Looking up, I'm relieved to see a long blue shirt sleeve and the gleaming silver badge greeting me. Leaning across the seat, I open the door and Lane ducks his head inside.

"Where's this carload of young stalkers?" He manages a wink before he looks at where I'm pointing over my shoulder.

"Under the streetlamp about six cars back. Green Civic, four doors."

As if on cue, the car's headlights turn on, blazing light on the road in front of it as the small team of women pull out of their space, back onto the road, and drive at a steady pace past us.

Lane bends over and pokes his head back into the car. "Well, that's taken care of."

"For now." I smile at Lane. "Thanks. I may be back."

"Any time. Welcome back, by the way. Saw Amelia last

week," he continues. "She said the house was finished now. Congrats, man. Having your home done right on time to light it up for Candy Cane Lane, that's epic. Good time to throw a housewarming party, get to know your neighbors, right?"

No, our street isn't called Candy Cane Lane. It's American Legion Drive, but for two weeks every year, it turns into Candy Cane Lane. The whole neighborhood, which consists of our street and three others, decorates their homes to light them up each night around the Christmas holiday.

It was Amelia's idea to build our home there, on the lake. Our dream home, so she could host friends at the holidays and go all out decorating each year because that is what she loves to do. Only this year, that gorgeous dream house will sit empty because neither one of us have moved in.

"I'll have to talk to Amelia and see what she has planned." No need for me to get into the nitty-gritty of my relationship with Lane. Considering he's the only person I really know here besides Amelia, it says a lot about me doesn't it? "I've not been around much this year, so she's in charge."

"Okay, well, let me know. I make a mean eggnog if you ever want to try some." Lane gives me a look, one that makes me think he may know what's going on, but then again he shouldn't. He stands up straight and taps the roof of my car. "Be careful out there; it's icy tonight."

"Will do," I say, as he slams the door shut.

With a wave, I'm back on the path to the bed-and-breakfast, my mind now casting itself back to the last time Amelia and I spoke. She didn't say a word about the house. It wasn't the best conversation: we'd argued a lot and I know I did my fair share of finger-pointing on that call. I'm man enough I can admit it wasn't my finest moment, but to have her send the divorce papers a few days later to punctuate her anger with me?

Ouch.

My phone rings on the seat beside me, not giving me any time to mull it over. The dashboard is connected to the phone, showing me the name of anyone who calls. Seeing the name of my assistant and best friend pop up helps soothe the worry in my gut.

"Hey, Bex, how're things going?"

"Things are good here, and you sound like a man who has surprisingly found some Christmas spirit," she says with a chuckle.

Seeing a familiar sign ahead, I begin slowing the car down and signal left as I turn down the road that will take me to the bed-and-breakfast. It also gives me the best view of the houses that are lit up on this side of Candy Cane Lane, minus one brand-new build, of course.

Yes. 'Tis the reason I chose this place to stay.

"A little. Judging by the Christmas decorations around me, the elves here have been busy." Bex and I have been friends for over fifteen years. We met in an acting class and have been tight ever since. It's good to have someone like her on your team in a town that's full of smoke and mirrors. She's like a fan: spinning and helping me clear the murk. Bex was in our wedding as my best man, and—no joke—she loves Amelia probably as much as I do. I'm worried that if Amelia and I do split up, I'll have to help Bex pick up the pieces as well as mend my own heart. "Are you calling to give me another lecture on how to win Amelia back?"

"You know I'll draw you a blueprint if you need it, but no, I'm actually just reminding you that you have a couple of interviews over the next few weeks we need to make sure you do, okay?" She pauses for a moment, probably ready for me to try to back out, but there's no fight in me. Not now, when I'm so close to a bed.

"I know you want to be considered 'off-grid' so you can work on things, but the studio phoned," she continued. "I've sent you an email with the dates, times, and contact deets for the folks who you'll be talking to."

"Bex..." Before I can start, she shuts me up.

"I'm doing everything I can to protect your time away. I know you want to focus on Amelia and the mess you've made."

Her honesty and lack of a filter are why I keep her around. "Thanks?"

"Don't thank me yet. The studio is pressuring me to make sure you show up for these interviews. So, I'm supposed to remind you that you signed a contract and that you are—"

"Supposed to be available when the time comes to do press junkets of any and all kinds. Yada, yada, yada, and a little blah, blah, blah. I know the spiel. If they get mad at you, send them to me." This is extra stress I don't need any time of the year, much less right now.

"I know, and I will." She goes quiet. Bex is the kind of person who is always bubbly and excited; it's why she makes such a good assistant. She's sunny, so it's easy to tell when her mood shifts because the storm clouds come and sometimes they can be gray. But when she goes quiet, I get nervous. "I know I promised I'd leave it alone, but can I say one more thing, Spencer?"

"Of course." Pulling into the driveway, I angle the car into a parking spot and turn off the ignition.

"I just want to say that I love you and Amelia like my own family. You two are couple goals for me. It's one of the things I noticed when you met her, the way she fit into your world, growing with you as you got more work, and then once you hit it big, how she held her own. She's one of a kind."

Bex is right: not everyone can live in this world, but Amelia did. She does. Amelia got it from the start because she understood the entertainment industry having worked in it herself for such a long time.

And I'm not going to let Bex's compliment go unnoticed. "Did you say we're couple goals?"

"I love that you choose to focus on that particular part of what I said," she says, cracking up. "It's because of how good you two are together. You both have always encouraged each other and empowered one another to go off and do your own things, but now, the way I see it, you need to find time to sit down and hash out these issues. One-on-one, *mano a mano*. Marriage isn't always easy. It gets messy, right? So, now you have to get in there and clean up the mess you made."

Ooof. She shoots, she scores. "Nothing like being hit with a truth bomb."

"Just go fix your relationship, and be on time for your interviews." She stops talking for a second before starting again. "Hey, I've got a call on the other line. I'll talk to you later."

The silence in the car is louder than any concert I've ever been to in my life. I stay seated here, getting colder, looking out the window. In front of me, the inn where I'll be laying my head at night. To my left, the neighborhood I should be moving into flashes all bright lights and happy feelings, the exact opposite of what I feel inside me at this very moment.

Closing my eyes, I take a second to steel myself for the weeks ahead of me. I'm here for Christmas with a mission. I've got work to do. Like getting my wife to fall back in love with me.

Again.

TWO

Amelia

"Are you sure you want to put this place on the market?" Sighing, Riley nudges herself closer to me as Dylan wraps an arm around my waist, holding me tight to her side.

"It's your dream home, Amelia," Dylan murmurs. "There's nothing wrong with starting the next chapter of your life here, is there?"

There shouldn't be, only there is. This house was supposed to be ours, the one I was moving into with the love of my life. It's the house Spencer and I have dreamed about for years, building it in our minds back when we shared a one-bedroom apartment in West Hollywood, when he was crossing his fingers and praying to get his next acting gig. Back before the work was starting to be steady and the paychecks matched the size of his dreams.

"Dream houses are for Barbies," I manage with a tiny snort. Not a snort of happiness, either. Turning around, I take in the open-plan kitchen and living area, complete with a deck outside that creates a feeling of space as it flows, taking the interior with it out to the exterior. It's perfect for the large family barbecues, holidays, birthday and graduation parties we had planned. Planned being the operative word here.

The sound of heels clicking on hardwood floors makes me snap my head in their direction. Etta pulls her hair back into a loose ponytail as she crosses the room, taking up space beside me.

She digs into my ribs with her pointy elbow. "Well, I, for one, am a *huge* fan of Barbie." As if to back herself up, she adds a visual, holding her arms open wide. "Enormously huge."

"Right?" Riley agrees, clutching a paper bag close to her chest. "How old is she and she still looks good."

"Honestly, that woman slays me," Dylan interjects. "She has her own car, a townhome, and a killer pool. Does she even have a job?"

"Who cares?" Riley giggles. "I had one of her pools when I was little."

"If I had to be any fictional character, I'd be Nancy Drew." Dylan punctuates the end of the sentence by pumping a fist in the air. "She's pretty cool—hanging out and solving mysteries with Bess and George...and I've always loved that one of her girlfriends was named that. Then I met a George. She goes by Georgie." Dylan's eyes bounce around, looking at all of us. "You guys know her. She owns the bookshop in town."

This is the side of Dylan that makes me happiest, freely thinking out loud. Beside me, Etta chews on her cheek in what must be an attempt to stop herself from laughing.

"Where are you going with this?" she asks.

"How long has Nancy Drew been around and she's still, like, eighteen years old?" Etta wags her finger at the three of us. "She's found the fountain of youth, that one."

"As much as I love this conversation," Riley says, shaking

the brown paper bag she's been clutching in her hands, "we've got food here that needs to be eaten and we have a house to christen...where is the champagne, anyway?"

We all look at each other quizzically before I remember I'm the one who has it. Grabbing my keys from my jacket pocket, I nod my head toward the door. "It's in the car and, judging by the temperature outside, should still be nice and chilled."

"It *is* super frosty for December, isn't it?" Etta walks over to the bank of windows overlooking the lake. Night is only settling in upon us now, and Christmas lights, probably set on timers, fire up and turn on, brightening up the homes around Lake Lorelei. "It's so cold, I bet it'll snow."

"Bite your tongue!" Although, waking up to a blanket of snow does sound kind of nice. Giggling, I jog out the door, down the steps of the porch, and head to my car. Grabbing the champagne bottle, I turn around to head back in but stop in my tracks when I see the house from this angle.

The entrance itself is a masterpiece with the old antique oak door polished to a rich mahogany sheen I'd found in a local secondhand shop. Flanking the entrance are floor-to-ceiling windows that have a slightly mirrored appearance on the outside, providing those inside with the freedom to look out without being noticed. The roof is adorned with weathered copper, its verdigris patina adding a touch of rustic charm to the home's otherwise modern and pristine appearance. Chimneys rise from the roof like silent sentinels, their bricks waiting to be mellowed by the years of sun and rain ahead.

The best part about where we built was finding out that our lot was part of what they call Candy Cane Lane. I was so excited. People come from all over the region to drive around these streets and feel their festiveness. Finally, my dreams of stringing lights on the house, decorating the yard to the hilt, and handing out candy canes to strangers driving by or walking the streets with hot chocolates, all of us merry and bright, would come true. Spencer and I would practice on our own for a year or two before we—hopefully—started our own family. Our kids would have grown up surrounded by community and tradition, and enveloped in our love.

At least, that's what I'd hoped. It was *the* fairy tale. My happily ever after, not just the kind in the movies.

Sighing, I push the thought to the back of my mind. There's no crying when it comes to champagne. Squaring my shoulders, I jog up the steps of the wide front porch, large enough to be another living area, and let myself back inside. Everyone is hunkered down on a large picnic blanket that's been tossed in the middle of the living room.

Flipping a switch on the wall, I'm thankful I've kept the power going as a bank of lights turn on over the fireplace, giving the bricks a warm glow. One of the ladies has put a playlist on and Michael Bublé plays in the background singing about a White Christmas. Fingers crossed that songs from *A Charlie Brown Christmas* come on next. I could use some moody and melancholy Charlie Brown tunes at this moment.

"Let me help." Etta scrambles to her feet, taking the bottle out of my hands. Riley and Dylan hold the red plastic cups we'd brought with us aloft, and we all giggle and clap as Etta pops the cork free from the bottle.

"Okay." Dylan holds her cup in the air. "Here's to your home. No matter what, it was a true labor of love, and whatever you end up doing with it—"

"She says she's gonna sell, Dylan," Riley hisses. "Leave it alone."

"I *said* whatever she ends up doing with it, Riley," Dylan hisses back, forcing an eye roll from Riley while Etta and I exchange a grin. Undeterred, Dylan clears her throat and starts her toast again. "Whatever may come—sell it, keep it, burn it down—we're here for you. You've been a rock-solid friend for all of us, but especially for me."

I can feel tears stinging my eyes as Dylan reaches over and takes my hand at the same time Riley and Etta snuggle up on either side of me and wrap an arm each around my shoulders.

"You've given us hope at times when we've needed it," Etta whispers, laying her head on my shoulder.

"And you've inspired us to do great things, make big moves, and to do it all with grace," Riley adds. "This little family we've formed? Ain't nobody going nowhere, unless we're together, got it?"

The power in a circle of friendship this tight is that it gives you fire. Sitting up a little taller, I hold my cup out in the middle of our group.

"Here's to all of us: we've gone our different ways to get here, but what matters now is that we're here. Together."

As if they'd planned it, all three cups smash into mine, and the four of us crack up as we hold them high above our heads and scream, "Together!"

We all plop back down onto the blanket, digging into the feast Riley brought for us to nosh on. As I start to enjoy a little brie spread across a very crisp slice of apple, Etta brings up the elephant in the room.

"Will you see Spencer this week for the reading of your aunt's will?"

Chewing thoughtfully, I nod. Don't want to bite my tongue. I search for a way to steer us off my least favorite subject, but it's an impossible one to avoid these days. Luckily, Dylan's got questions that are not about Spencer.

"Your Aunt Hattie sounds like she was a fun lady. Did you know she was sick?"

Shrugging a shoulder, I finish chewing, surprised when a

bit of apple peel gets stuck in between two of my teeth like a door jam. Using my tongue, I manage to dislodge the peel and get immediate relief.

"She told my mother and her closest friends, but she didn't want anyone to worry. That's how she rolled. She was super independent, traveled all over the states in her RV for the last ten years or so." I smile at her memory. "She always did her own thing, and she did it well. One of her favorite sayings was, 'Life is like a rental car. Get behind the wheel and floor it!'"

"How come the reading of the will is just for you and Spencer and not in, like, a group?" Riley asks.

"My mom and sister already saw a family lawyer in Maryland and sorted their inheritance before they left on their big European trip." Taking a sip of my champagne, I place the cup down on the floor beside me. "Since Spencer and I are both named in the will, and he planned on coming back anyway, we decided to hear it together."

The room goes quiet...and all through the house, not a creature stirred.

Nope. Not even a mouse.

"So," Etta begins slowly, "is this the first time you'll be seeing Spencer in person since he left last year?"

"Kind of. We've had a few calls, a lot of texts, and roughly eight video chats that didn't end well." I pick up my cup again, fingering its rim. "He flew in last night. We spoke briefly this afternoon and decided to meet for breakfast tomorrow." A sigh I can't hold on to any longer escapes my lips. "I need to call upon the powers of all the women in my family who have walked this earth before me to get through the next forty-eight hours. A will reading *and* seeing Spencer."

I'm still staring at my cup. I don't have to look up to know there are three sets of eyes watching me like hawks right now. Or maybe more like elves on the shelves?

Dylan swallows. "Does he have the...?"

My "Yes" comes out a little more sharply than it needs to, considering Dylan's got nothing to do with the doom surrounding my marriage. "Sorry. Yes. I had him served not long ago just so we could start the process when it's time."

"Are you sure you're ready to go there?" Etta asks, her hand covering one of mine.

I feel like I'm in quicksand, everything around me blurred and fading. Taking a breath, I squeeze Etta's hand and pull mine back, using it to reach across the blanket and swipe a grape off the plate.

"All I can say is...the resentment is real, you guys."

Etta looks shocked, her jaw going slack. "And what pray tell does he have to resent about this whole situation? He's the one who left."

I cast my eyes down sheepishly. "I didn't say he was the one who was feeling resentful."

Etta's eyes, once flashing with darkness, widen with knowledge. "Ohhhhh."

"I've spent the last year checking in with myself, and the one conclusion I keep coming to is that I'm mad. We moved here so it could be my time. We spent a long time building his career, with me taking an executive role at a studio to help keep the stability. He always said when I was ready, he'd step back so I could do my thing."

"And when you do your thing, it's amazing," Dylan coos. "A rejuvenated campground with shopping, wine, and an event center, plus the art gallery you two opened—"

"I know," I interrupt. "It was my time, but more importantly, it was also supposed to be *our* time. Together." Picking up the red plastic cup, I hold it close to my lips and bite the rim in aggravation. "He said he wanted what I did. To start a family."

Closing my eyes, I take another sip of my champagne.

When I open my eyes again, my friends are all exchanging worried looks.

"Hey, stop it, you guys." Putting my cup down, I wave both hands in the air. "We're not going here, not now. This is a celebration because, hey, I built a house!"

"Which is epic," Etta agrees, smiling. "I just wish your mom and sister could have made it."

"Me, too. But they've had this two-month trip to Italy and France booked for ages. They'll be back next year in February, and they're already insisting on coming here for, like, a month to be with me."

"Well," Riley begins, "not in replacement of but complementary to the women in your family, we, your fellow Fab Four members..."

"Is that what we're calling ourselves?" Dylan interjects. "Isn't that the term for Wills, Kate, Harry, and Meghan?"

"Oh, not good." Etta shakes her head. "They're not even talking anymore, right?"

"Stop it, you guys," Riley exclaims, clapping her hands together. "It's because we're like royalty. We're awesome alone, but together, we're superheroes. And that's something I can toast."

Riley puts her cup back in the air, narrowing her eyes as she glances at the rest of us. Almost daring us to disagree.

"I can toast to that." Etta chuckles, putting her cup up in the air one last time. "To all of the superheroes out there who don't wear capes."

Dylan nods. "To the power of friendship and to the wonderment of a new year ahead."

I pause for a second, thinking of what to say. When I have my words, I add my cup to the small cluster. "To growth, change, and to better things ahead!"

A cheer of happiness fills the air around us. I may seem

buoyant and am smiling on the outside, but it's a stark contrast to the internal war percolating.

Deep inside, there's hurt. Confusion. But these women fill my soul with hope.

Things have to get better. Right? I mean, it is almost Christmas, after all. A time of miracles and all that.

What's a girl got to do around here to get a miracle?

Spencer

Opening my car door, an icy blast of fresh, crisp morning air hits my skin and, man, it feels good. Living in Southern California is amazing if not for the weather alone, but over the years, it's given me a skewed version of what seasons are supposed to be.

It's funny to think I've missed the winter. Snuggled down in my bed this morning, with the heater going and lost in my dreams, I'd almost overslept. Luckily there's someone who does have an alarm staying in the room next to me—and when that alarm went off, we all heard it.

Grabbing the baseball hat from the seat beside me, I hop out of the car and slam the door before checking my watch. One thing I know for sure is that Amelia will be on time—she always is. That's one of the traits I love and admire in her. She insists it's best to be somewhere ten minutes early so she can breathe easy and know she's where she needs to be, especially when she can't find a parking space or is stuck in traffic.

Me? Well, I was perennially late when we first met, but her enthusiasm to be the first to arrive eventually rubbed off on me. Glancing at my watch, I would pat myself on the back, but even though I'm early, I'm willing to bet my savings she's already sitting inside with a cup of coffee in her hands.

Eggs Over Easy is the newest cafe in town, at least according to the @secretsofsweetkiss's Instagram page. Bex texted me the info last night, making sure I knew where I was going. I even had a chance to look at the menu before I got here, which I'm sure she took into account. She knew how nervous I'd be seeing Amelia in person today.

I slide the baseball hat on my head before I get out of the car, making sure to pull it down so my face is somewhat shielded by the brim. Sweetkiss Creek is one spot where, barring the stalking carload of teens the other night, I've been able to blend in without any issue. The folks here who do know who I am or what I do don't really care...at least they don't seem to. And it's a breath of fresh air. Do I get the occasional person asking Amelia if I can autograph something for a school auction to help raise funds for the new gym they want to build nearby? You bet, and I will always happily oblige.

Swinging the door to the restaurant open, I'm hit with a wave of heat as its warmth rolls out to greet me. I park myself beside the "Please wait to be seated" sign and cast my eyes around the bustling cafe, the smell of bacon hitting my senses and making me drool. The rumble in my stomach tells me I've not eaten enough. It's a sound I'm used to these days; my appetite went out the window the minute Amelia and I said the words "trial separation."

I drag my eyes around the room, searching tables for her familiar face. It can't be that I beat her here. There's no way. My gaze lands on a table along the back wall, and in the corner, a familiar smile greets me. It might be the dawning of one, but it's a smile with a few teeth and I'll take it. Amelia waves, pushing her chair back and standing to give me a hug as I approach her table.

This is the longest we've gone without seeing one another

on a regular basis. We've spoken but kept it brief. We kept our distance, as she asked we do, but seeing her standing in front of me now and smelling the scent of her perfume sends a current of prickling shivers across my body. It's a familiar feeling, but there's something in this hug that I can't put my finger on.

Shaking off my inner monologue, we embrace with me admittedly hanging on a little longer than I should in the middle of a restaurant, but I don't care. Holding her now, I fight the urge to press my face into her hair and pull her even closer. The hit of jasmine and citrus is like caffeine for me, my heart racing as I close my eyes and inhale her. I've missed this woman, but admittedly, some barriers have been erected—and not by myself—since we last saw each other in person.

We take our seats as the waitress drops off a large cappuccino with no foam in front of me. I drag my eyes to Amelia's, losing myself in their doe-like depths, and smile.

"My favorite. Thank you." Leaning forward, I reach across the table to take her hand, which she snaps back. I'm not prepared for that and it stings.

Amelia must have seen the hurt register on my face, but she pretends not to as she hands me a menu.

"They have the best omelets around." She leans forward and taps her finger next to one called the Protein Pile. "That one is all you. Stuffed with veggies, a little bit of turkey and cheese of choice, with a side of bacon."

A flash of warmth lights up my insides; she hasn't forgotten. I feel like it's a small sign that she still cares, and maybe there's a chance. Should I tell her I already picked out that same meal when I looked at the menu online last night? I place the menu on the table in front of me and turn my attention to my coffee. In my haste to get out the door, I'm not too shy to admit I'm way under-caffeinated for this part of the day.

"Done, that'll be my breakfast, then." I take a few big sips of my drink while she scans the menu. Funny thing is, I know she's not studying it to figure out what she wants to have, because again, I know her. How do you think I got into the habit of having Bex send me menus for any meals out? Amelia either already knows because she's been here before or she would have looked at the menu online before coming. That's what she does "for efficiency" and it makes sense.

Sipping on my coffee, I watch her twirl a piece of her hair on the end of a finger with one hand while her eyes slide along the menu as she reviews the selections. Watching her like this now reminds me of our first morning together after we got married.

She'd laid on her side, tangled in the bedsheets with me, laughing as we went over every moment that we'd loved from the day before. The sun wasn't even awake yet, its rays were just peeking through the window of our suite, and she'd laughed and twisted a piece of hair as she recalled the moment my guy best friend Levi had taken over the dance floor with Bex, getting the whole party to do the macarena.

Unbeknownst to our guests, I saw an opportunity and had taken that moment to pull her into the coat closet, holding her close and firm against me, and running my hands across her body, starting at her fingertips and working my way up her arms. I can still hear the gasp escape her lips when I leaned in, pushing myself against her—my lips tasting her neck from the moment...

"Excuse me?"

Snapping back to attention, I turn toward the voice and find a young boy suddenly standing beside our table. I know the look he has on his face, and judging from her patient expression, so does Amelia. It's usually at times like this that someone wants an autograph.

Ever the patient wife, Amelia dips her hand into the bag sitting on the bench beside her and pulls out a pen which she slides across the table to me. I turn sideways in my chair so I can face the little fan and grin.

"Well, hi there. How are you today?"

One tiny shoulder lifts in a shrug. "Good, I guess. My mom's making me go shopping."

"Well, it's good to spend time with your mom. Are you picking out Christmas gifts?"

Biting his lip, the little boy nods, his eyes flicking from mine to Amelia's and back again. His nervous energy hangs in the air around us, or it could be ours, but no time to discern what's what now. Poor guy. I can tell he's having trouble asking me for my autograph, so I lean in a little closer and swipe the pen from the table.

"I'm Spencer. My close friends call me Spence."

This small gesture seems to put him at ease. "I'm Daniel."

"Nice to meet you." Daniel stares at his feet, moving his weight back and forth from one foot to the other, swaying like a clock's pendulum. "Well, Daniel, would you like me to autograph something for you?"

Ignoring me, he keeps his hands shoved in his jacket pockets when he turns around and looks across the restaurant in the direction of a table whose occupants are watching him closely. A woman, who I assume is his mother, waves hello before blushing and looking away. Glancing quickly at Amelia to check in, we exchange a knowing smile.

Turning back around, his green eyes cut my way as he pulls his hands out of his pockets and puts several chocolate bars on the table.

"Oh..." Confused, I look over at Amelia for help, but her eyes dance with glee like she and this kid are in on some secret that I never got the memo for. I quickly deduce she'll be no help, so I busy myself by picking up a couple of the candy bars and turning them over in my hands. "Am I signing these for you?"

"Oh, no." The little boy's head shakes back and forth adamantly. "We're selling these as a fundraiser for our school. Would you like to buy some?"

I'm pretty sure my jaw unhinges as Amelia's laugh cuts the sound barrier. It hits a pitch that could break glass. Lucky for her, it's infectious, and I've missed her, so I can forgive it. Reaching into my back pocket I pull out a twenty-dollar bill.

"How much are they?"

"Six dollars." Daniel grins. "Each."

What kind of highway robbery is this? "What are you raising funds for, to go to the moon?"

"Spencer," Amelia manages through gritted teeth. "Give him the money so we can have some chocolate."

Handing over the money, the little boy does some fast math. "I can get you change, and here"—he slides three candy bars my way—"these are yours."

I chew on the inside of my cheek so I won't laugh. "Keep the change."

"Cool," he says with a grin that stretches from ear to ear, showing us missing front teeth. "Thanks, mister!"

We watch him walk back to the table at the front and the adults there pat him on the back and congratulate the little snake oil salesman on his sale. Grinning, I turn myself back around so I'm facing Amelia, only to find her watching me.

She trawls her gaze across me, as if appraising an antique or studying a document. "It's good to see you, Spencer."

"You've seen me, we FaceTimed." There I go. It's a talent. Deflecting with humor of the obvious.

"You know what I mean." Amelia rolls her eyes. "In person. Here. In Sweetkiss Creek. It's nice to have you in the flesh."

"Well, it's nice to be here." I look around the small room and back to Amelia. "I guess you're settling into this little town now?"

If I were to judge things by the way her face twists, I'd realize something I said or the way I said it didn't land well. Those beautiful lips that were beginning to turn up at the corners are suddenly drawn tight, closed like curtains on a blustery and cold winter's day.

"Yes, you could say I'm settling into the 'little town' now. In fact, this little town has been really good to me over the past few months as I've fumbled about and made it home." She makes sure to meet my gaze, most likely so she can drive home her last word for effect. "Alone."

Point made. Touchè. And all that jazz.

I hold my hands in front of me in surrender. "I'm not trying to start anything before we have breakfast, Amelia."

"Did I hear someone say breakfast?" A waitress with a syrupy sweet Southern drawl is suddenly standing to my right, pen on her order pad. Looking up, I see by the name tag that Vivian is ready for us. We place our orders and turn back to our standoff once she walks away.

"Look, I'm sorry." Some of the wind has blown out of Amelia's sails, thank goodness. I'll chalk that up to Vivian's timing. Amelia reaches up and frees her hair from its ponytail, shaking her honey-blond locks loose. As much as I'm conflicted about where we are in our relationship, all I want to do is rake my fingers through her hair and...

"Are you even listening to me?"

No, no I was not. I was too busy thinking about your hair, Amelia, and pressing my face into it. Slowly, I shake my head and, judging by the exasperated sigh, can sense she had been telling me something important.

"Oh, Spence." I detect some sarcasm as she leans back in her seat and crosses her arms in front of her chest. "I'm glad to see these months apart have done us a world of good."

Is she jumping to being defensive a touch early? I'd say so, but am I going to be the one to tell her that right now? No, I'd rather give a cat a bath, thank you.

"I'm sorry. I'm here and I want to talk to you. It's obvious we've got a lot to figure out, don't we?"

"We do. I feel like a lot has been shoved to the back burner for us to deal with later. But the water in the pot is boiling now."

There's a euphemism there, that much I know.

"Amelia, I hope you can see that my being here means I want us to figure things out between us." I take a quick sip of my coffee, trying to think of the right words to say to get it across to her that I'm here for the right reasons. "Honestly, it should be obvious to you that I'm here to make things right."

When I look at her, it's quite clear that those were *not* the words she was looking for.

Uncrossing her arms, she leans toward the table, dropping her voice to a loud whisper. "What's obvious to me is that you checked out at some point. Somewhere between 'yes, I'm ready to take a step back from acting and start a family' and 'I'd love to get my acting career back up to full throttle again, come what may!'" She throws her hands in the air. "How did you think that was going to make me feel?"

"I wasn't trying to throw a cog in the works." I don't think I was. At least not at first. "I took the job so we would have more security, more financial stability for a family."

"You took the job so you could keep on acting." She shakes her head side to side with vigor. "You took the job because you didn't want to move here, Spencer. I'm sensing a little bit of Peter Pan syndrome happening. It's more fun to be the boy who never grows up, isn't it?"

For the second time this morning, my jaw unhinges. At the rate I'm going, I'm gonna need to wire it shut. "Is that what you really think?"

"I have only the evidence laid out before me to go on. We

decided to make a change, we got here and started settling in to find our way, and then...poof! You're off. We've, well, I have lived here for almost a year and you've actually been physically here maybe five times for a total of, what, maybe three or four days each time."

I resist the urge to shake my head and act like I have water in my ears. "What are you saying?"

"I feel like we're not on the same page and this conversation is evidence." Amelia sighs, slamming herself against the back of the booth. "I'm saying that you've not given this 'little town' as you call it a chance."

Ouch. Her words are like a sucker punch to my gut and the air quotes don't help. "That's unfair, Amelia."

It feels like a cold front has come in, moving past all of the other tables, finding its way to ours and settling in directly above us. We sit, staring each other down, her mouth set in a tight line, and me, here, with my stomach doing somersaults.

It does that when I'm busted, and she's right. I never fully landed in Sweetkiss Creek the way I said I would. I tried to do the right things to get more involved. I insisted we buy the art gallery in town because it needed direction, and an injection of fun and true art, so I took it on as my project. When she found the campground and had her big idea to buy it and turn it into a cool little compound for tourists and locals alike, I got behind her and cheered her the whole way. But, the whole time, I had one foot semi-firmly planted back in LA after I promised I wouldn't.

Smoothing her hair back, she sits up a little taller. "I don't think it's unfair. I feel like you used the press we kicked up here to help fuel your re-imagined acting career. Good headlines, right? Former heartthrob actor and ladies' man turned domestic, Spencer Stoll, has moved to a small town in North Carolina to live there, ladies and gentlemen. How cool is that? He's a man who wants to step back from the limelight and is going to bring a little more life to this small corner of the world."

"Sarcasm is not your color, Amelia."

"No. It is, however, my new love language," she manages dryly before hanging her head and blowing out a huge breath of air. "I promised myself I wouldn't do this. You just got here; we don't need to go over everything right now."

We sit in silence for a moment, eyes locked on each other and unmoving. There's more going on in the unsaid right now than in what's being said, and sometimes it's good to let those silent conversations happen.

"Changing the subject." Amelia clears her throat and attempts a smile. "Did you know the house is done?"

A pit forms in my stomach. The house we had planned together, our dream home. It's the house where we wanted to raise a family, to have Christmas. The house where we'd grow old together. It was the house I was supposed to be overseeing the construction of but had pawned that off on Amelia, like everything else, so I could go back to Los Angeles and back to acting.

I'm unmoving as the waitress reappears, sliding our plates in front of us. Looking down at my plate, I realize my appetite has decided, once again, to take a time-out.

Something beeps loudly, like R2D2 from Star Wars, and Amelia grabs her bag, shoving her hand inside. R2D2 does his thing again as she pulls her phone out. I was the one who put that sound on her phone for her so she'd giggle every time she got a text, but there's no hint of a smile or even a chuckle now. Glancing at the screen, she reads it quickly before placing it back in her bag and pushing the chair away from the table.

"There's an issue at the art gallery—you know, the gallery you were going to run?—and I need to go in for a bit." She gets up, tossing a business card in front of me. "The main number to the gallery changed. This is the new phone number if you need to reach me there."

Something else I'm not aware of when I would have known before. How much am I out of the loop on these days?

I don't want her to leave, but I don't want to force the issue either, so I nod. "Can we catch up later today?"

She shakes her head. "When I'm done at the gallery, I have to go by the campground. There's an event there this week, so..." She shrugs, looking sheepish. "I guess I'll see you tomorrow at the lawyer's office. After the reading of the will, maybe we should discuss how we want to navigate the rest of our conscious uncoupling. It would be nice to have that figured out before 'the most wonderful time of the year' kicks off."

Amelia's use of aggressive air quotes does not escape me. The irony that Mariah Carey's "All I Want for Christmas Is You" comes blasting over the sound system at that moment is truly fitting, but then again, so is her anger with me.

I watch as she stops at the waitress station to get her food to go, then flounces out the door without so much as looking back my way.

I've done this, I know I have. I made promises and I didn't live up to them.

And I'm going to need to pull more than a Christmas miracle out of my butt if I'm going to win her back.

FOUR

Spencer

The tiny inn, which had felt quaint and delightful when I arrived, feels counterintuitive to my mood when I walk in the front door after my breakfast with Amelia. Looking around the giant living room, just one of two spacious shared living areas, it looks as if one of Santa's reindeers regurgitated pine needles and holly across it, spraying the mantle, the side tables, and even the bay window. Granted, it's tasteful regurgitation, but still.

The lights on the giant tree in the center of the enormous bay window twinkle. On closer inspection, I'm pretty sure each branch has something hanging from it. There's a familiar rumbling sound at the base of the tree as a train set boasting a sign reading "Christmas Express" does loops, going around and around. Much like the cafe where I sat not long ago with Amelia, there's Christmas music playing in the background, only this music is soft and classical and soothes my nerves.

Amelia's words were like a million tiny scissor kicks to my gut, but I deserved to hear every word, whether whispered or screamed, that she had to say. I've not been able to shake off a few of her best hits, and there's one that I need to own up to and take accountability for because she *is* right.

Driving back from town, I looked at Sweetkiss Creek with new eyes. It's not that big, really; I can find my way around but don't know it like she does. I've not spent time here so I have no friends to call up and go have a coffee or a beer with, and I barely know the place. I put my name on an art gallery and then left, leaving her alone to deal with things. To start another business on her own and oversee our dream home being built. A home that, if I don't fix this, we'll never live in together.

Sighing, I spy the remote for the television. A quick look around tells me I'm alone, so I plop onto the couch and press power on the remote as I do.

The television comes to life, and the opening scene of *Love Actually* flicks across the screen. It's the scene where people are at the airport and greeting loved ones. I'm a huge fan of this movie and not ashamed to say that one of our Christmas traditions is turning it on when we decorate our tree. This scene is one of the best parts in my opinion. Amelia's, too—she's always had a fascination with airports and watching people come and go. We have a game where we make up stories about the people we watch, giving them personalities based on appearance or how their energy is, which could be based on the speed they walk or if they're a loud talker when they're on their mobile phones.

My heart bangs in my chest; I need something else to watch. I can't do this right now, nope. No matter how sticky things are with us, we save this film for our time. It's part of our tradition. I'm going to hold on to hope that I'll be decorating something with her this year, because Christmas isn't over yet.

I buzz past channels trying to find something I can zone out to for a few minutes. I finally land on another holiday film, but after a few seconds of watching, I realize it's one of mine. A holiday film I'd done years ago for Hallmark. Smiling to myself, I remember talking to Amelia about this particular script. It had come along at a time when I wasn't sure if I wanted to keep going, if I was still passionate about acting. My dad sent the script over with a note advising me not to do it, but he wanted me to read it anyway. Amelia read it first and loved it, so she's the one who made sure I read it. When I was done, I couldn't wait to talk to her about it. A holiday movie about a small-town cop who pulls over his ex-girlfriend, the one he'd broken up with at prom, the day she arrives back in their hometown for the holidays? It was a rom-com, which my dad didn't want me to do, and all I could think was if Amelia liked it, then sign me up. It was an instant hit and it's played every year at Christmas now. I hadn't done this one for the paycheck, I did it for Amelia because she loved the script so much.

Sighing, I let the remote drop onto the couch beside me as I close my eyes and press my fingers to my temples, massaging them. Willing my brain to give me guidance, but all I can think about is her.

That woman. She's everywhere.

The sound of someone clearing their throat behind me makes me jump. Spinning around in my seat, I'm surprised to find a tiny older woman dressed as a cross between an elf and one of Santa's reindeer grinning madly at me.

"Well, my husband told me not to let you know that we know who you are, but..." She inclines her head in the direction of the television. "Since you're sitting here watching yourself on TV, I figure I can say something now."

"Oh." Swiping the remote, I press "off" faster than you can say Blitzen. I can feel the heat rise as my cheeks flush. "I'm trying to find something, anything, that will take my mind off the holidays."

"Well." She looks down at her outfit before casting her eyes around the room. "Since it looks like Kris Kringle just vomited all over our house, I guess we're not helping."

A crack of laughter comes out of me, and it feels good. I lean forward and place the remote back on the coffee table. "I think it looks great. I don't mean to come off as such a Scrooge. You should probably ignore me."

She chuckles. "Would you be able to ignore you if you had *Entertainment Magazine*'s Sexiest Man Alive in your living room?"

My already hot cheeks grow hotter. I move my line of sight down to stare down at my feet, embarrassed. "Oh, boy."

"Come on, let me tease you some, son. It's not often we have a celebrity in our midst." She peers at me over wire-rimmed glasses. "I'm Mrs. Miller, I run the bed-and-breakfast with my husband. But you can call me Diane." She cocks her head to one side, her gaze tight on me. "Shoot, aren't you supposed to live in that house on the lake y'all have been building this year?"

Small towns. Nosy people.

Play it cool, Spencer.

"I am, but..." I begin slowly, hoping the words will come while I silently pray for an interruption. "My wife and I have some very strong, and very different, opinions about the house at the moment, so—"

"So you're staying here while you work on these...opinions?" She clicks her tongue against the roof of her mouth. Wise eyes meet mine, and I can tell I'm not getting anything past this one. "You know what they say about opinions, don't you?"

Okay. I think I may know where she's going with this. I may not be a local, but I've played them on TV and I know when someone is about to take the other person's side. Diane is most certainly Team Amelia. I'm searching for the best response possible when a man in a Santa outfit walks in the room. I do a double take, but thankfully I recognize him from checking in the night before.

"Diane, leave Mr. Stoll alone. I told you not to meddle." He wags his finger at her before kissing her cheek and nodding his head toward the back of the house. "Your cookies will come out of the oven in a moment. You may want to check them; it smelled like something is burning back there."

As if on cue, a buzzer goes off from somewhere in the back of the house, and Mrs. Miller winks at me before running from the room, like a middle-aged Christmas fairy, the faux reindeer antlers bouncing on her head.

"Don't worry, I'll save you some, Spencer," she calls out over her shoulder as she pushes the swinging door open that leads to the kitchen. "In fact, I'll put some to the side for you and you can give them to that gorgeous wife of yours. My cookies are known to make love—"

"Okay, Diane." His cheeks flushing red, Mr. Miller puts a hard emphasis on her name, causing her eye to twitch. He sniffs the air, probably for good measure. "I think it's a fire now."

The pair exchange a silent moment—Diane narrowing her eyes at her husband, but glancing sideways at me and smiling —before she finally disappears from sight. Thank goodness.

"Sorry. It's a small town." Crossing his arms in front of his chest, he nods his head my way. "She's a fan of Amelia's. Your wife helped us when our home flooded earlier this year. She heard about what happened and called us up immediately to invite us to stay out at the campground for free in one of those nice refurbished cabins until we got things fixed."

The smidgen of underlying attitude I felt coming from Mrs. Miller makes sense now. "Amelia's the best."

"She sure is. Very giving woman." A pair of dark brown eyes bore into mine like an unsaid line was being drawn. Mr.

Miller uncrosses his arms, rolling up his long red sleeves. The whole time he keeps my gaze. "We've all grown quite fond of her since she moved here."

Again, there's a feeling I've dipped my toe into something that's akin to boiling water. Unwittingly, I've made a reservation at Team Amelia's hotel and I'll be lucky if I survive the night.

A ding in my pocket breaks the silence of the room. Swiping my phone from its hiding place, I'm relieved to see Bex's name flash on the screen before me. I look woefully at Mr. Miller and wave the phone in the air.

"I need to take this. Please tell your wife thank you for the cookies, but I'm actually trying to cut back on sugar..."

"Oh, that's fine. They're not for you. She wants you to give them to Amelia." He looks at me, a smile finally breaking across his rugged features as he winks. "Her cookies brought together feuding neighbors over in the next county, who were fighting over a hedge. It got ugly, with one guy running his tractor through the hedge to make a point. But in the end, Diane took her cookies over and made them share a plate and talk it out."

Mr. Miller looks so happy to be giving Amelia cookies, even if they are getting to her by proxy, that I don't have the heart to tell them she's gluten free and probably won't be able to eat them.

"Oh, and don't worry. We know Amelia's gluten free. She told us when we had dinner with her last week." His grin gets wider while his eyes narrow a touch. Not a lot, but enough. "Diane reworked the recipe just for her."

It's fair to say we've entered a territory I'm not familiar with at all, and the fact my city-fied wife has blended in so easily here honestly shocks me. Should I be used to people knowing my business with my face splashed on almost every magazine that's out there? Yes, I probably should. But most of the time the magazines aren't printing the truth. I say most, but really 99.9% of the time, it's made up or they go off of "a source close to Spencer confirms" gossip reporting, when that source is someone I worked with years ago when I was a waiter and they don't know me or my life now.

But this? This time it's someone standing in front of me who doesn't know me, but they know my business and my wife's—and it's off-putting because it's the truth.

And the truth hurts, you guys. Like stubbing your toe right after biting the tip of your tongue kind of hurt.

"Well, I know she'll appreciate that." My phone, thankfully, begins ringing again. Holding it up in the air like a trophy and I've won first prize, I backtrack from the room, heading back to my suite. "Please tell Diane that I'll be happy to take the cookies to Amelia. Thank you."

Mr. Miller calls out "Sure enough," but I'm already up the stairs with the phone pressed tight to my ear.

"Sorry, Bex," I manage, unlocking the door to my room and ducking inside. "I was sidelined by the people who own the inn. What's up?"

"What's up?" She sighs the sigh to end all of sighs ever, her breath slamming into my ear. "Have you not seen any media today?"

Now that she mentions it, no, I haven't seen anything. I've not looked online for news and it's not like I've had time to sit in front of the television. I tried that and look where it got me.

"I'm blissfully unaware. Why?"

"Someone saw you the night you arrived."

That's no big deal. "At the airport?"

"No." She pauses. "They took pictures of you going to the bed-and-breakfast and checking in."

"Okay, no big deal. Right?"

Her silence tells me otherwise.

"Bex?" I quiz her. "What does it say?"

She takes a moment, probably to brace herself for bracing me. "The story that goes with the photo is that your marriage is over. The headline says, 'Spencer Stoll spends holidays alone after cheating scandal.'" She pauses, probably to let it sink in, but she goes on. "They've put photos here of you with your co-star from the film you just wrapped. Look, they've used some pictures that to the casual observer look really bad."

I feel sick. "What do you mean really bad?" I blurt, perplexed.

"Well, I know these are from the movie—they're ones the set photographer took for the director. But, of course, the photos the reporter got their hands on are the ones where you're snuggled up in front of a fireplace for one of your scenes, and another one where you're dancing really close together and about to kiss."

I can hear my heart beating like a bass drum in my ears. I've been through this before and so has Amelia. It's not the first time a smarmy member of the press or some paparazzi-wannabe has tried a stunt like this. Sadly, it happens more often than most folks know. We've had people try to climb over our neighbor's fence in the past to get a good photo of us in our backyard by the pool. One of the best smoke-and-mirrors moves they attempted was getting photos of me by the pool on Sunday afternoon with "another woman."

We were home one night, about to leave for a costume party, when someone showed up at our door. They actually had the gumption to walk right up and knock. When Amelia answered, he showed her the photos of me, outside, hugging a woman with long blond hair. When I joined her at the door, we stood and let him think he was intimidating us until Amelia opened up a bag that was slung over her arm, pulling out the blond wig accompanying her costume and showing it to the photographer.

We'd laughed our butts off…right after she slammed the door in his face.

But, this time it's different. Back then, we were united and not apart for very long. It was us: her and me against the world. This is the first time they've done this kind of nastiness when Amelia and I have not been in the same state for over a year.

"Hey," Bex said on a hush. "You still there?"

"Oh, yeah." I croak back to life, winded, like I've been slammed in the stomach by a heavyweight fighter. "Can you call the team handling press for the film and ask if they can release all of the photos taken from set?"

"That could mitigate some damage." Bex's tone tells me she's in thinking mode. "I'll call them right when we hang up and see if we can throw a press release together as well. All press is good press, right?"

"Ha." Her attempt at humor fails miserably on me.

"The other thing I'm thinking," she goes on, "is that you need to warn your wife. She's been down this road before and knows how to handle things, but—and I know it's a big 'but' with everything you two have going on—that was then, this is right now. It would be good for the two of you to make sure if you're out together, public-facing in any way, that you look happy."

I'm about to object, but Bex interrupts me before I can start. "Before you freak out, this isn't some romantic comedy where the movie star needs a fake girlfriend. I'm saying you two, you and your very real wife whom you are still married to, need to mind your Ps and Qs. Don't fight in public, don't even argue or correct one another. Don't fight to pay a bill if you're out to eat. And if you start to bicker, make sure you stop it. De-escalate is now your middle name. Got it?"

"I've got it." And I do. Bex is right. "Be aware of our

surroundings. And ignore anything that shows up in the press."

"Good man. Wait, hold on." There's a pause before she hops back on the line. "The PR team just texted. They're all over it and offering to release the pictures, so crisis averted."

"Until the next one, right?" Shaking my head, I lay down on my bed and close my eyes. "Thanks for the heads-up."

Five minutes after I've hung up with Bex, I allow myself to doze off, willing visions of sugarplums to dance in my head.

FIVE

Amelia

Even though I've looked at it a million times already, I check the time on my watch again. Tapping its face, I look up apologetically at Mr. Greenspan and shrug my shoulders. Albeit, it's an irritated shrug, but it's all I've got right now.

"I told him to be here at ten, Mr. Greenspan."

Mr. Greenspan gives me his kindest smile. "It's fine. It's only five minutes after."

As if on cue, the phone on his desk beeps and his assistant's hushed voice is suddenly in the room. "Umm, I've got..." Here's where she drops her tone dramatically, whispering, "*The* Spencer Stoll here to see you, Mr. Greenspan."

"Send him in, Sheila, and please, try to not ask him for an autograph, will you?" He chuckles, shaking his head as he taps a button on the phone to disconnect. "She's a bit of a fan."

Great. Of course she is. Everyone is a fan of Spencer Stoll, except for Mrs. Stoll, that is. After reading that ridiculous story about him and his co-star on HollywoodHeadline.com this morning, you think I'd be sitting here spitting venom about my husband, but I won't. There's absolutely no need.

Why? Because this comes with the territory and because I know him. He may not have been around for me the way I wanted him to be this past year or so, but I know without a shadow of a doubt he wasn't spending time with anyone else. Except Bex, and she's okay in my book.

The door to Mr. Greenspan's office swings open, and Spencer breezes through it holding a small cardboard tray with three large coffees securely held in the carrier. He holds it up for us to see like it's a medal he's won.

"I know I'm late, but I brought coffee." He may be speaking to the both of us, but he keeps his eyes trained on me. "Large vanilla soy latte, extra hot?"

"Thanks." Reaching out, I take what he offers, but admittedly I'm watching him through veiled lenses. "Saw the story this morning."

"Oh." Spencer's shoulders drop and a look of sadness washes over his features. "I was hoping you wouldn't. I've already been on the phone with Bex about it."

"I figured. Are you getting the film to release all of the photos taken on set?" I take a sip of my coffee, placing it on Mr. Greenspan's desk in front of me as Spencer tilts his head in a yes.

"They're on it." Tense shoulders hiked up to his ears suddenly relax as they slide back into their usual position. "We can talk more about it later?"

I nod my head, but honestly, we don't have to talk about it. However, I know it'll make him feel better. He always worries about me and how I'll handle his fame. It's cute of him to do, and actually really thoughtful, considering that I get swept up into fake headlines sometimes with him. Someone told me after we got engaged that I needed to be a strong woman with a back made of steel so I could handle what comes with him and his career, and they weren't kidding.

"Gotta love a small town," Spencer says as he steps up to

the desk and places a cup in front of Mr. Greenspan, who is parked in his chair on the other side. "Carly, at the coffee shop next door, said this was your favorite. Large latte with a splash of hazelnut, half-caf?"

Mr. Greenspan's smile swings free as it grows from a half-grin until it's, quite literally, stretching from ear to ear. I didn't even know this man had teeth.

This, my friends, is what I like to call the Spencer Effect.

"Why, thank you kindly, son," Mr. Greenspan manages, his Southern drawl sounding a bit thicker than it did a few moments ago. I look around the room, making sure I've not been dropped into some kind of parallel universe. Nope. Still in the lawyer's office.

Spencer grabs his coffee from the tray and makes himself comfortable in the wingback chair beside mine. Turning my way, he winks and holds his coffee in the air as if he's toasting me.

Rolling my eyes, I tilt my head to one side to look at him better. "You know, this is a will reading, Spencer. Not an award ceremony?"

"Come on, now." He crosses his right leg over his left and puts the cup to his lips, taking on a swagger akin to Matthew McConaughey. "I'm just happy to be here."

Even Mr. Greenspan cranks his neck in surprise, cocking his head to the right as he squints his eyes and takes Spencer in.

Seeing his reaction, Spencer backpedals, uncrossing his legs and sitting up tall in his seat.

"What I mean is, I'm just happy to be here. In Sweetkiss Creek." He then turns his sole attention back on me. "With you."

I have no idea what's going on with this man right now. Turning away from his absolutely odd gaze, I wave a hand in the air. "Can we please begin? I have an appointment I need to be at soon."

Between us? I don't have an appointment, but these two don't need to know that.

Taking a sip of his beverage, Mr. Greenspan all but groans with erotic enthusiasm over his coffee. "Good coffee, Spencer. Do you know what beans she used? I swear it never tastes this delicious."

"I think she said it was a Jamaican blend? I can find out and let you or that sweet assistant of yours out front know." Spencer holds his cup in the air to toast Mr. Greenspan. "Good though, huh?"

Aaaannndddd, we're back in the alternate universe. Giving up, I slam myself into the back of the chair and take another sip of my coffee, wanting to hate it so I can spit it out all over the carpet. But I can't do that.

They're right. The coffee is good. Really good.

"Okay," Mr. Greenspan says as he places his cup down and grabs a folder on his desk and waves it in the air. "I've got the copy of what your aunt has willed the two of you here."

Placing the folder back on his desk, he flips it open and scans the documents. Bless his heart, he starts squinting to the point he has to pull the papers right up close to his face, using his forefinger as a pointer.

"Ah! Here it is." He sits back and pats his left shirt pocket. Feeling out what he's looking for, he slides a pair of readers out and puts them on. Begging the question why he didn't put them on before, but I'm not going to ask. We've wasted enough time already.

Silently, he reads over something, then peers over his glasses at me, his gaze bouncing to Spencer, then back to me. The way his face twists makes something inside of me a bit twitchy, but I've been known to read into things.

"Everything okay?" I ask, leaning forward and putting my coffee on his desk.

"I think so. If you like RVs."

Spencer and I look at each other and back to Mr. Greenspan. "RVs?" I query.

"Listen to what it says right here. 'And to my niece, Amelia, I leave you my beloved RV. It's done me well over many miles and I know she has more to go.' Then there's a note that it's in Sarasota Florida for you and Spencer to pick up." He puts the papers down and looks at the two of us expectantly.

"What was that?" Spencer and I say in unison.

"You've been given an RV."

"An RV?" My thoughts jumble. "Okay, I guess I can arrange to get it in the early part of next year…"

"No can do." Mr. Greenspan holds up a hand to stop me mid-thought. "There's another note, an addendum about a time factor. It needs to be removed from storage sometime within three weeks after you receive the news. So, you need to be there by"—he flips through the papers on the desk, finding what he needs—"by…oh. By Christmas."

Someone pick me up off the floor. "By Christmas? We need to go to Florida now, to get this thing?"

He nods, looking back and forth at the two of us. "It's most unusual to have something with this tight of a turn-around, but yes. It's been stipulated that you have to get it within a certain amount of time. If you don't pick it up, you forfeit any right to own it. It'll be sold at auction."

"What?" Spencer finds his voice beside me. "This is insane. Did Aunt Hattie really do this?"

"I have no idea," I say, turning to Spencer. The thought of being in a soup can with a bed, for days on end, is far from thrilling for me. Not just with Spencer, with anyone. I am not a fan. "Surely we can hire a service to pick it up and bring it to North Carolina. Like towing it or on a flatbed or something?"

Spencer nods his head in agreement as Mr. Greenspan

shakes his head, tapping the paperwork in front of him. "It says *you* need to pick it up."

"Okay, well..." My mind races. "This is impossible timing. It pains me to say it, but I think we should just have it auctioned off and I can send you your half—"

But Mr. Greenspan continues to shake his head. "It would appear that your Aunt Hattie added a note to this particular part of her will. If you and your husband do not collect it and drive it back to North Carolina together, the RV will be sold at auction and the proceeds will go to a local charity."

"I can live with that." I look at Spencer. "We don't want an RV."

Spencer holds up a hand. "I do."

Well, there's a plot twist I didn't see coming. "She's not your aunt."

"But she left it to us."

"I'm her blood relative, Spencer. I should have the say in what we do with it."

"I've always liked that RV, and you know it." Putting his coffee down on the floor by his feet, he crosses his arms emphatically in front of his chest. "You're freaked out by it. Admit it."

Freaked out at the possibility of a forced proximity situation? One hundred million percent. "Stop talking, Spencer. Let's not do this here."

"Wait just one moment. There's more." Obviously having enough of our shenanigans, Mr. Greenspan clears his throat and takes the floor. "The will goes on to stipulate that once you arrive on Siesta Key—what a nice name for a town— you'll be given keys and an envelope with further instructions. But if it's not the both of you, there will be no handing over of keys, no instructions and, as I said, no RV."

"Fine." I know it's her last will and testament, but some

things you have to bypass. "Do we at least get to pick out the charity the proceeds will be going to after the auction?"

"Um, hi." Beside me, Spencer wriggles in his seat, putting his hand up again. "So I don't get a say in this at all?"

"Nope," I begin, before catching myself. "Well, actually, you can help choose the charity."

"I'm not done yet, Amelia." Mr. Greenspan's eyes move quickly over the will as he reads something, taking his glasses off before he sits back into his chair and massages his temples. "It would also appear that your aunt has left some valuable family heirlooms and other items that are for you, Amelia. But you'll only get them if you go get the RV and drive it back."

"What?" Aunt Hattie was always a bit quirky. Some might say eclectic, others a brick shy of a load. But this is not like her. At all. "This is insane and feels emotionally manipulative. I can't just take off and go get an RV right now."

Turning to look at Spencer, I feel like he should be sitting there ready to back me up. He, of all people, knows how much there is to do. But there's a smile on his lips and a glint in his eyes I've never seen before.

"I think it's amazing," he says in a breathless voice as he looks over at me. "Your aunt has given us a mini-vacation."

How on earth does he see this as a mini-vacation? "A forced one."

Spencer sighs. "Why can't you simply have an adventure?"

"Adventure?" I throw my hands in the air. "I'm on one already. It involves selling our house and dividing our property, Spencer."

"Look at this!" A squeal of happiness erupts from Mr. Greenspan. "There's some good news."

My head snaps his way. "Please, I could use some good news right about now."

"She's even paid for your plane tickets. You just need to tell me when you want to leave, and I'll book them ASAP."

"That's your good news?" I'm gonna scream.

Mr. Greenspan closes the folder and crosses his arms in front of his chest. "Amelia, if you don't go, your aunt has given permission to the people who have your heirlooms to keep them and do what they will with them."

Opening a side drawer in his desk, Mr. Greenspan brings out a manilla envelope and slides it over his desk toward us. I can see our names scribbled across its front.

"What's that?"

"No clue, but my instructions were to give this to the two of you when I saw you."

Shooting Spencer a look, I grab the envelope and rip it open, pulling out more paperwork. Flipping through the documents, I'm hoping there will be a letter in here or a note from Aunt Hattie saying "Ha ha! Got you!" and we'll find out this is all a joke. A weird prank.

Thumbing through the items, I don't find a letter. No note to me, no "Ha ha, fooled ya!" cards. How could she do this? Of all people. I'd spoken at length to her this year about my issues with Spencer and how it's affected me. She, of anyone in my family, knew what was going on with our marriage and the frustration I'd been feeling.

Spencer leans over and taps the papers on my lap. "So, what's in the envelope?"

I start holding things up in the air for him to inspect with me. "We've got some maps."

Spencer opens one of the maps, and then another. "I thought she'd have written something here, but nope. Just maps."

Pushing the maps to the side, I pull out a smaller beige envelope, this one thick and full of more paper. Tearing it open, I'm wondering if a wad of cash is going to spit its way out at me, but instead, I find the paperwork for the RV and a hand-drawn map labeled "Siesta Key." There's a word, *Cinch*, highlighted in green at the bottom of the page.

With nowhere else to turn, I look at Spencer, but he's no help. His lips twist into an evil grin as he laughs. Funny enough, at this moment, I need the reassurance of that laugh of his.

"I think Aunt Hattie has planned something for us," he muses. "That woman loved her bingo, a quiet afternoon to knit, and a good scavenger hunt."

His words put a skitter in my pulse. "How do you know this?"

"She told me. Remember that time I was filming in the Ozarks, in Missouri? She was nearby, on the road in her RV, and stopped for a day to see me."

And I do remember. She was really excited to go to a working set and see how a movie was made. She had called me that night and had gone on and on about how she was treated so well, and that Spencer had made sure she had access to craft services, the folks who make all of the yummy food for the cast and crew, and as much as she wanted. It made me giggle how she called it crafty, the term used on set by those in the know as an abbreviation for the heart and soul of all the things: the food.

"So, Cinch is a person," Mr. Greenspan interrupts. This man must think he's dealing with two people who are at least twenty bricks each shy of a load at this point. "He's been storing the RV in Sarasota for Hattie. He'll make sure you get access to it once you arrive. But, like the rest of this inheritance, there's a condition."

Spencer and I look at each other and back at the lawyer. His look, full of hope. Mine? Untrusting.

I could hear my heartbeat buffeting my eardrum. "Of course there is. What is it?"

"You can't stay there. You'll fly into Tampa, then drive to

Sarasota to pick up the RV, and after that, you need to get on the road. This order comes from your aunt. Also"—he taps the folder again—"Spencer's right about the scavenger hunt part. She's given Cinch an envelope that he'll hand over to you with the keys. It'll give you instructions on where you go next."

"Can you tell us anything else?" I'm all but begging here.

He shakes his head. "Just that she asks you both block out at least seven days for the trip and"—he slides the documents back in their folder and takes his glasses off, eyeing us both—"she wants you to trust her."

Looking over at Spencer, I find him wearing a grin that could rival the Cheshire cat's.

Seven days. In an RV.

Making eye contact with Mr. Greenspan, I roll my shoulders back and sit up a little taller. I can do this.

"Okay." My eyes bounce from his to Spencer's, locking there. Spencer's crystal-blue eyes sparkle with joy, and the crinkle around their edges remind me of how I used to love staring into those eyes of his and getting lost in them. "I know she wants us to take seven days, but I want to get back as fast as we can. It *is* Christmas."

"I know." Spencer nods, reaching across to squeeze my forearm, an intimate move that sends a wave of shivers across my flesh. "Then we'll make it happen. For the spirit of Christmas and all that."

Sensing his sincerity, I nod as well. Trusting him and trusting my deceased aunt, who is somehow controlling this excursion from her grave. "Okay. Let's do it."

Just us. In an RV.

Ho. Ho. Ho.

SIX

Amelia

"Do you really have to leave in two days?" Etta tosses another basket of freshly dried clothes on the bed for me, and I reach in to snatch out one of the bath towels, smelling it. I love the smell of clean laundry. "And are you sure you're only going away for a week, because it looks like you're packing for twelve."

Looking at the piles of clothes scattered around the room, she's not wrong. "I figured I should bring anything I may need. I have no idea what I should pack for an RV trip."

"Well," Etta says as she reaches over and grabs one of my lace nighties and holds it against her, "are we thinking this will come in handy?"

"You never know. I may need to use it as a flag to wave down a passing motorist if we're on the side of the highway." Swiping it from her grasp, I toss it back into my "maybe" pile, ignoring her smirk. "I don't know. Barney was the easiest to pack. Dog bed, leash, food, and we're done."

"Don't worry buddy, she's going to pack your outfits, too." Etta scoops up Barney, my sweet little Beagle and bestest bud for the last few years, and snuggles her face into his ears.

"He's so soft. I'm glad he gets to go with you. I'm still happy to watch him—you know Thor and Hercules love him—but I feel like he needs to be there for emotional stability."

"Mine or Spencer's?" Winking, I hand her the bag I've packed Barney's necessities in and point to a drawer in my bedside table. "I keep his sweaters and little jackets in there. Can you grab a few out, and please pack for all seasons. We're driving from Florida, and who knows what kind of weather we'll hit on the way back."

"At least you start in sunny and warm," Etta points out, opening the drawer. "You should take your bathing suit, just in case."

Cracking up, I point to the large suitcase splayed across the bed. "Oh, it's in there. Along with an outfit for any occasion."

Peering into my bags, Etta squeals as she plucks one of my Louboutins from where they rest. "You're taking your Mary Jane 'Pumppie Wallis' heels with you? Where do you think you'll be going? I doubt the RV is big enough for a ball, Cinderella."

"Oh, stop it." Snatching them back, I put the shoes in their bag and close the suitcase. "I told you, I need to pack for every occasion, Etta. I can't just throw some things in a bag and go, I need to know I'm prepared for anything."

"I'll let you slide this time," Etta responds, shaking a finger at me, "but if you get teased by your...what are we calling Spencer? He's still your husband, but—"

"But what?" A grunt comes from below, and looking down, I find Barney staring at me expectantly. Bending over, I slip into a cross-legged position on the floor, allowing for him to curl up in my lap and snuggle against Mama. I like the heat of his little warm body, too; it's reassuring.

"So, I've got more questions. Don't shoot me." Etta closes her eyes and flinches like I may hit her. "Have you guys had any time to talk about the d-i-v-o-r-c-e papers you sent?"

"You don't need to spell it or tiptoe around it." I stare off into space as I massage Barney's back. "No, we haven't talked about the divorce papers, there hasn't been time."

Etta's lips curl upward and her eyes light up. "Until now."

"Until now." Sighing, I hang my head. "Considering we'll be roughly two feet from each other the whole drive back, I'm guessing we'll have plenty of time to chat it up."

"I wonder why she said for you to take seven days and not just try to drive it as fast as you can? It's only an eleven-hour drive from Sarasota to here," Etta muses. "I looked it up."

Grinning, I'm reminded why I love this woman so much. Of course she looked it up. I've done the math, too, I've been on Google. It's a straight shot from Florida back to Sweetkiss Creek for the most part, but it all depends on where Aunt Hattie has us stopping for these heirlooms I need to pick up.

"Knowing her, she wants us to take our time, but why stick us together when she knew we were having problems?" In my lap, Barney snuggles a little deeper as he takes a giant breath and sighs it out, falling into a puppy sleep while I massage the spot between his eyes.

"She probably made the will out before she got sick and never had a chance to change it." Etta shrugs. "I think it's cool she planned out a whole scavenger hunt for you. Sounds like she had a sense of humor."

"She really did. She'd have to if she expects me to want to spend more time than I need to in a five-by-five box with the man I'm maddest at right now." Meeting Etta's eyes, I give her my brightest grin. "We have to take in account that we're not driving a car, it's an RV, so we'll need to stop more often for gas. I'm pretty sure we won't be able to drive as fast as we normally could if we were in a car, plus we have the unknown variables of stopping at a few locations at her request." My stomach flips when I think about how unspecified this whole trip is. "And we won't know where those stops are until we get to Florida, so we can't plan too far ahead. Which is killing me."

"You know, if you think about it, this is actually kind of cool," Etta says as she squats on the floor beside me. "Your deceased aunt is sending you on a treasure hunt. It's the East Coast and not in the Caribbean, but it's gotta be a little bit exciting."

"I mean"—a grin slowly dances on my lips—"it's not horrible, right?"

"Right!" Etta throws her head back and howls with laughter. "I think it's amazing and I wish we could put a hidden camera in that RV to see what happens. You guys would be the best reality show."

"Bite your tongue. If I find any cameras in there, I'll know who made it happen." Shaking my head, I lean back against the bed. "I'm just praying I don't lose it on him at some point."

"Please." Etta rolls her eyes as she leans over to caress Barney's paw, which has flopped over my leg and dangles above the floorboard. "You can't even ask him if he has the divorce papers. You're packing like you want to impress, and he's making sure you're okay after a story breaks accusing him of cheating. Yeah, you guys are toast. Oil and water. Opposites attract and all that."

"You actually suck. Take my side will ya?" I swat her arm playfully and stop trying to suppress the giggle that's formed in my throat. But, if I was to go off the knocking that is happening in my gut, there's some truth to her words. "It is good to have him here. To see him in front of me."

Etta's elbow hits me in my ribs. "See? I know you've been busy building a wall, but you two need to talk. I think this is the universe's way of making sure that nothing is left unsaid."

"Could be. Or it's the universe's way of making sure we break up as soon as we can." I toss both hands in the air.

"We're being forced into this situation, Etta. I'm not prepared."

"What?" Etta gasps dramatically and clutches her heart. "The great Amelia has flaws? Well, I'll be." She throws an arm around my shoulders. "Honey, something tells me you weren't prepared when you met Spencer—I know I wasn't with Zac. I can only imagine that getting married is a whole other ball of yarn, isn't it?"

She watches me until I nod my head in agreement. Holding her gaze, I fight the tears that threaten to fall. Instead of letting them go, I choose to close my eyes and take a few deep breaths. I need a second before I can open them again and look her way.

Her words have hit me like a ton of bricks. Being married is different. I mean, of course it is. I took a vow the day I said I do, and it's one I want to stand by—but if I can't see eye-to-eye with the man who is supposed to be the love of my life, then I don't know what to do. Seeing him for breakfast, as weird and uncomfortable as it was, I can't fake the way my body reacted to seeing him.

When he walked into Eggs Over Easy, it was like I was seeing him again for the first time. Forgotten, for the moment, were the arguments and the loneliness of the last year. When his eyes slammed into mine, I wanted to cross the room, jump in the air, and throw my legs around his waist and tell him to take me home, right that very minute...but, no. Instead, I'd waved, given him a little hug, and then found multiple ways to take digs at him.

But, let's flip the coin. I have my reasons to be mad. He told me he wanted to step back from the limelight and work on us, on having a family. He wanted to be with me, supporting me and cheering me on. "It's your time to shine" is what he said. Exact words.

A loud beep makes my eyes snap open. Etta points to my phone on the floor in between us. "Is that a new text tone?"

Picking up the phone, I see it's not a text but an alert. I'd put a small wireless camera in the window by the front door so I can see who's there if someone knocks, but I'm not expecting anyone. Since it's a rental, I didn't want to pay to install anything permanent, so this little camera was perfect for me.

Tapping the icon, I open the app and flick to the "live" button. Surprise, surprise. I flip the phone around to show Etta. "It's Spencer."

"Ahhh," she says with a smirk as she stands up. "Time for me to make my escape."

There's a knock at the door, followed by Barney doing his Beagle job and *york, york, york*-ing (that's the way his bark sounds, I'm not being silly) all the way to the front hall.

When I open the door, Barney all but flings himself into Spencer's arms, making little grunting noises of happiness. I can't be mad at this, these two are quite cute together. It was Spencer who had picked Barney out for me all those Christmases ago, after all.

"Barney!" Spencer is on the floor, ruffling Barney's fur and laughing. "I've missed you, buddy."

He drags his eyes up to meet mine, beautiful blue eyes framed by long eyelashes are smiling at me, causing me to gulp for a steadying breath of air. My hand flies to my chest, which feels tight. As I drag a sip of air into my lungs, Spencer stands up, reaching out and laying his hand across mine. In a few quiet moments, I'm able to resume my normal breathing pattern again.

I want to scream. He causes such a reaction inside of me, yet his touch feels like hot fire on my skin. WHAT IS EVEN HAPPENING?

He steps back, his hand still covering mine where it lays on my chest. "Hey."

"And hello to you, too, Spencer." Etta steps around from behind with her winter jacket already zipped up snug around her. "Don't worry, I'm not staying. I'll leave you two to chat about your excursion. I need to get going to meet Zac. We've got his work holiday party tonight, and I can only imagine how crazy the Sweetkiss Creek police department can get once they've had one eggnog too many."

She squeezes my arm as she slides past me, and I'm impressed that she manages to nod curtly, but cordially still, to Spencer as she disappears out the door and into the night.

We stand in the doorway for a moment more, his hand lingering on top of mine, before I pull it away and clear my throat.

"I'll make us some hot tea." Fighting the shiver that ripples across my body, I head toward the kitchen, not surprised when I turn around and find Spencer and Barney both hot on my heels. The sight makes me laugh. "So it's a family meeting, is it?"

"I like hearing that." Spencer's eyes light up.

"Calm down." I shake a finger in his direction. I fill the kettle with water and put it on the stovetop to heat up. "And also pace yourself. We've got days alone together, so I'd like to keep our arguing to a minimum if we can."

"That's fair." He leans against the counter, watching me.

"So." The cabinet I need to get into to get our tea bags is behind him. I nod toward the cabinet, and he steps to the side, arms crossed but still keeping his eyes on me as I'm rustling around inside it. "You were acting weird today."

He sighs. "The story that broke threw me off my game."

"You can't fool me. I've seen you navigate worse." I hold up a selection of tea bags. "Peppermint, chamomile, or chai?"

"Peppermint, please." He shifts his weight from one foot to the other. "If I was acting strange, it's because I've discovered that the town of Sweetkiss Creek pretty much hates me."

"What are you going on about? No one here hates you."

"Oh, they do." Spencer shrugs his jacket off but not before pulling a small package out of one of the inside pockets. He places it on the counter in front of me. "Your number-one fan Diane Miller sent her gluten-free Christmas cookies for you. If I don't go back and tell her you ate them, she's going to kick me out of the bed-and-breakfast."

"You're being dramatic," I say with a chuckle. I've always liked Diane. "Wait, are you saying Diane hates you?"

Spencer nods. "Among others."

"Who else?"

"Well, Etta left here pretty quickly after I showed up."

A low whistle begins, coming from the stovetop as the kettle begins to sing. "She wants to give us privacy."

I grab two mugs and put the tea bags in, taking the kettle off the stove and pouring the water. Out of habit, I grab milk from the fridge and add a splash to Spencer's with a spoonful of sugar, too, then slide it in front of him. As I do, his finger snakes out and he runs it over the back of my hand.

"Your friends don't like me," he whispers.

"Well," I whisper back, "they don't know you."

We stand close together, looking at each other. I feel him in the room, like a force field. This man can take up space in the most frustrating and yet the loveliest of ways. He's in my heart, my mind, and now, after a long time apart, he's in front of me. He's tangible. And he looks amazing. I forgot how his jaw clenches when he's thinking, and it sends tiny little fluttering kicks through my system.

All I want to do is fall into those arms of his and have them wrap around me. I want to forget all the promises that went by the wayside, and I want to start again. To be us. To be what we were or what I thought. I want to let my fingertips dance their way along his biceps, and feel him holding on to me, big protective arms wrapped around me, promising me we'll be okay.

Shaking it off, I step away from that tractor beam of a gaze and, signaling to Barney, head into the living room to the couch. Spencer joins me there, where we both sit with our hot cups of tea and look at each other.

"So."

"So." I stare at my feet. "I take it you brought the paperwork with you?"

Spencer's face clouds over as I realize Etta's right. I can't even verbalize the D word, not to him.

"Yes," he manages through slightly gritted teeth. "I brought them."

Nodding, I move the mug from one hand to the other. It's hot and needs time to cool. I want to put it down on the table, but it gives me something to hold on to. "Should we talk about it?"

"You just said we should pace ourselves." He takes a sip of his tea, pulling it back quickly with a start. "Ow! That is hot."

"Must be how they coined the phrase 'hot tea.'" Leaning back into the couch, I choose to ignore the sideways glance he tosses my way.

"Must be." He leans forward and puts his mug on the coffee table, turning in his seat so he can face me fully. "Sorry, again, about that article. I'm not a fan of the timing."

"Makes two of us."

"You know it's something I can't control."

"I do, but it doesn't stop it from still making me feel bad when it's published and out there." I put my mug down on the coffee table. "At least it didn't make it onto the @secretsofsweetkiss Instagram account. Or to your dad's TikTok."

Spencer rolls his eyes. "I still can't believe he has one. It's ridiculous."

So, let's be clear: Spencer's dad is not a fan of mine. Never has been, probably never will be, and I have no clue why. Scratch that, I have my opinions why, but I keep them quiet. I was taught to respect my elders, even if they are on TikTok.

"As long as he's out there living his best life, right?" Yeah, I'm searching for something positive to say so I can stand by my "I respect my elders," but it's like Aunt Hattie used to say: If you don't have anything nice to say, then shut your lips. This is yet another dent in the armor that is our marriage.

Spencer goes quiet, the expression on his features telling me he's thinking the same thing I am.

"I'm sorry that he's such a hard person to deal with," he says, clasping his hands together. "I wish he was different, but he isn't."

"Hey, I've had enough therapy now in my life that I can look past some of his little digs over the years." It's true. A little piece of my heart actually aches for his dad, knowing their backstory. "Your mom leaving him when he was at his lowest really did a number on him. Look at how it's not only dominoed onto us, but into his own personal relationships, too. That man has the busiest dating calendar of anyone I know that is in their late-fifties."

"Yeah, it's kind of weird to know my dad is on TikTok, but when I found out he was on Tinder"—Spencer grins—"I almost passed out. He matched with Bex."

My hand flies to my mouth. "No. You're joking."

"I kid you not."

Leaning forward, I crack up, reaching out instinctively to grab his hand, and he's there, his fingers wrapping around mine as we share a laugh. My eyes rock down to where our hands are intertwined, and then I pull them back to his before clearing my throat to break the moment and pulling away.

"Um..." I stand up, taking my cup with me. "Do you need something? I need to finish packing and do some things before I crash."

Ignoring the way his features darken, I busy myself with straightening the kitchen. Spencer grabs his mug and takes a big swig before crossing the room to place it on the counter, then stands beside me as I fold some tea towels.

"I wanted to see if you were okay. I didn't like that I was accused of cheating, especially when we're...you know." He flips his hand back and forth between us. "This right now."

"Well, all is well here on the island of misfit toys. I'm fine." Yeah, Amelia, the outside is great. Maybe if I keep saying it out loud, I'll start to believe it, too.

"Okay, well..." He looks at his watch. "I'd better go back and pack myself."

"If you think of anything we might need, let me know." I incline my head toward the bedroom in the back. "You know I've packed everything, as usual."

"She runs a tight ship, ladies and gentlemen, but she can't pack to save her life," he says with a wink as he opens the door. He stands in the doorway, looking at me. "Good night, Amelia."

Closing the door softly behind him, he leaves. Grabbing my phone, I tap the app for my security camera as fast as I can so I can watch him as he walks down the steps and to his car. I even watch as he gets behind the wheel and pulls out.

I'm telling myself that it's just me, making sure he's gone. But in reality, my heart is slamming against my chest and I'm alive with a thousand hot pokers stabbing my insides.

Are we like toys that are broken and tossed to the side, to maybe be repaired or possibly thrown away? I've spent a lot of time praying we can work things out, but the way we're going we'll be bickering all the way to the courthouse. Or at least, all the way up I-95.

The part that makes me craziest? It's the part where I'm beginning to realize that I still have feelings for him. Not just feelings, emotions. And big ones. That man who makes me want to pull my hair out and scream. The man who makes my tummy skip with pure happiness some days, but can also make it clench up with irritation others.

This trip. Two people who aren't getting along being tossed into an RV. It sounds like the worst reality show ever.

I just hope we both make it back in one piece.

SEVEN

Spencer

"Is Barney comfortable back there?"

Straining against her seatbelt, Amelia turns around to check out our only child, who is currently in the far back seat of our taxi and dressed, against my better judgment, in a camouflage top.

"Looks like he is," she says, sliding back around so she's facing forward again. "Who would have thought Aunt Hattie would make provisions for Barney as well?"

"I'd say I'm surprised he also had a ticket, but it's like she's thought of everything. But I am surprised you didn't pack Barney with the kitchen sink and whatever else you have in three suitcases. We're pretty lucky we were able to get a taxi that's a minivan. Who brings that much baggage on a road trip?"

Judging by the huff next to me, that came off a little sarcastic. I don't have to look at her to know that those beautiful lips of hers are pulled tight as a drawstring bag right now.

"I don't know, Spencer. Please, tell me exactly who would bring their baggage on a road trip?"

"Ah, touché." Looks like the drawstring loosened some.

The flight from Charlotte to Tampa Bay was a quick one. By my calculations, if we'd been traveling light—key word here being light—we'd have gotten to Siesta Key by now and would have been on the road toward home.

But someone had to pack for every occasion. The same someone brought all the suitcases that had to be checked. As karma would have it, there was an issue when we landed with getting the bags in from the plane, and we had to wait close to ninety minutes before Amelia got her luggage.

She's quiet. Too quiet. I glance in her direction to see if there's any further reaction only to find her with arms crossed, staring out the window. Her jaw's set, her cheeks are flushed, and she looks a bit flustered. I forgot how gorgeous this woman can be when she's irritated with me.

"Hey." Amelia snaps to attention, interrupting my thoughts as she points at a sign up ahead. "Look, Siesta Key, next exit."

Our taxi pulls off the highway, following the signs pointing us to our final destination. It's only a matter of fifteen minutes more before we're turning off Route 41 and onto Midnight Pass, the road that will take us onto the small island, or key, to meet Cinch. I wind down my window to smell the salt in the air and close my eyes. I'm a salty-hair-don't-care type of guy and this little island seems like my kind of place.

Judging by the draft flowing through the car, I'm not alone in my idea to crack a window. I look across at Amelia again and find her doing the same thing, and it makes me smile. Out of habit, I reach over and squeeze her knee gently. I'm not prepared when her hand closes on mine and she squeezes back, turning my way with a huge grin on her face.

"Okay," she breathes. "This *could* be a fun adventure."

Wait a...who's this? I'm not going to second-guess myself

or question it; I'm going to hold on to the fact that at this very moment, she's calling this whirlwind an adventure.

We've not gone far when Amelia tells the driver to slow down. Clutching the directions from Mr. Greenspan, she points to a street sign ahead. "Take a right up here at Turtle Beach Campground."

Pulling into the small communal village, tents dot the coastline, scattered amongst the protection of the trees. Our driver maneuvers expertly into a parking space by the campground reception office, which is next to an old RV sitting on cement blocks, covered in brightly colored dots and chunks of beat-up tinsel and what looks like solar-powered Christmas lights.

No sooner have we parked before Amelia jumps out, Barney by her side. Shrugging her shoulders my way, she starts walking toward the ostentatious RV trepidatiously and leaves me to settle things with our cabbie.

Outside of the RV, in a small fenced-in yard of sorts—a yard filled with what appears to be old bicycle parts, some random tires that have been painted bright colors acting as garden beds, and a near dilapidated swing set—an older woman is dressed in a loose kaftan and wearing the most outrageous sunhat I've ever seen. She's busy hanging laundry on a makeshift clothesline, which protrudes off the RV, and eyeing Amelia she stops with her hand in midair. Her eyes narrow as Amelia walks toward her, her mouth set, but all of that seems to melt away as Amelia gets closer.

I feel like I'm in Wonderland. *Curiouser and curiouser.* When the older woman squares her shoulders and turns around, it's the first time I'm thinking Amelia may need backup. I hop out and open the trunk of the car, swiping my baseball hat from the side pocket of my overnight bag, and slap it on my head, careful to pull it down to cover my eyes. The air may be cooler than it is in summertime, but the sun here is beyond intense.

Jogging quickly across the dusty space—which is a bad idea in this humidity, let me tell you—I'm by Amelia's side when she stops in front of the woman's gate.

When I join her, the woman eyes us both a little more warily, her eyes falling to Barney, who sits at attention with his head cocked to one side, watching her as well.

She crosses her arms in front of her chest, narrowing her eyes again. "Y'all lost?"

"Pretty much," Amelia says with a laugh, which is a little more higher-pitched than her usual comfortable laugh. I know this laugh. It's the one that appears when she's nervous and not able to control a situation. I've been the cause of that nervous giggle before, so you can bet I know it well.

"We're trying to find a man named Cinch." I'm met with a blank stare. Maybe she didn't hear me. "It's Cinch, rhymes with grinch."

"Oh, I heard you." The woman knits her arms across her chest even tighter, as if she's a castle guard and she's been tasked with closing the moat behind her.

"Sorry, we've literally just flown in this morning from North Carolina. We're on a bit of a Christmas mission." Amelia hands Barney's leash to me, freeing her hand so she can pull out a folder in her bag. "My aunt sent me here to meet Cinch." She pulls a photo out of the folder and hands it to her. "I have no idea if you ever met her, but this is her. Cinch has something for me that I'm picking up at her request."

An expression similar to relief washes over the old woman's features, her suntanned face etched with the miles she's walked. It breaks into the most glorious grin I've ever seen. Popping a hand onto her hip, she angles her head to one side as she looks Amelia up and down.

"Well, you are 'Melia, aren't you?" The accent, a blend of

South meets Louisiana Bayou, has a sweet cadence. "We've wondered if you'd come."

She looks at me over Amelia's shoulder as if she's taking me into her confidence. "We get really busy here around Christmas; didn't want to miss y'all if you were coming."

A feeling of relief washes across me. "Oh, we made it."

The old woman's features soften as she visibly relaxes. "I'm Claire. I knew Hattie from her stops here to see Cinch." Claire flicks her wrist to her right, indicating toward another campervan, this one rather long and with its wheels but covered in more rust than paint. "That sad shack of a camper-van, the one with absolutely no holiday decorations? That's Cinch's place."

"So he really is a grinch?" I joke, wanting to eat it back when Amelia backhands my chest with her left hand.

"I'm sorry for my husband, Claire, he's got loose lips."

"He's right," she snorts. "That man is a menace. Like a seagull. He comes out of his shack every now and then to squawk at us, go to the bathroom, and then he's off again. You know..." Claire holds out her arms, pulling them into the air as she molds her hands into something that resembles claws. Drawing her right knee into the air, now balancing on her left leg only, she bends my way and looks me dead in the eyes as she opens her mouth, peeling back her lips to reveal a set of teeth straight from the set of a horror film. "SQUAWK. SQUAWK!"

Beside me, Amelia bites her lower lip, her shoulders shaking, a sign she's doing her best at holding her laughter in.

"I was told I need to see him," Amelia presses on. Good on her, I wouldn't be able to. "I'm supposed to get something from him."

"Yes, you are!" Claire exclaims, putting her leg down and winking. "Your RV. Go on over and knock, he's in there."

Amelia winds her way around Claire's RV, through a

makeshift art installation that has been made up of thousands of broken bottles all attached to old pieces of wood. There are no sharp sides, all of the glass is smooth and it reflects the light, sending it scattering across the ground around us like thousands of tiny diamonds twinkling and swirling.

Ahead of me, Amelia all but leaps up the steps of the tiny trailer to knock on the door.

The door swings open, letting out a tiny blast of cool air. A disheveled man stands in the doorway, eyes blinking like he's just woken up. He's got his silver hair pulled up into a tiny man bun on the top of his head, and his old University of Florida T-shirt looks like it could use a replacement.

Seeing Amelia, he steps outside into the sunlight, his tanned skin glowing almost bronze. The color he's rocking is the same color a lot of people I know pay good money for from a spray tan, but he's got it naturally. Gotta love Florida. The Sunshine State, alright.

"Can I help you?" he grunts.

Amelia pulls out the photo and explains to Cinch who we are. As she finishes, much like his next-door neighbor, a warm smile cascades across his features as it registers who we are and why we're here.

He grins at both of us, nodding his head and rubbing his chin. "Wow, you're a dead ringer for your auntie, you know that?"

"I've been told." Amelia shifts her weight from one foot to the other. "We're really sorry to bother you, but I'm here to get her RV. Apparently, she left it here with you?"

He nods, tilting his chin in the direction of where we drove in. "It's parked across the way, waiting for ya."

Turning his attention to me, Cinch gives me a good once-over, his eyes dragging the length of my body from my shoes to my hat, and then he whistles. "You're not one for this life, I can tell." He points to my shoes and guffaws. "Leather shoes?"

"I told him the same thing," Amelia commiserates, bonding with this man over my flair for fashion. She's one to talk. I'm pretty sure she packed a pair of heels for this trip, and I'm still trying to understand why. "Look, we can't stay long. We've been told we need to get this envelope from you and get on the road, so..."

"Oh, yes." He chuckles, stepping back inside his RV but still talking to us the whole time. "Your aunt said you'd want to get down to business real quick once you got here. Let me get it and then I'll show you the RV. It's a good thing I took it for a drive yesterday and filled it up with gas for you—your lawyer emailed and said you'd be here this week sometime."

We hear what sounds like papers being shuffled, the *thud* and *thunk* of what could be a box, maybe, falling, followed by a loud "Ah ha!" Obviously finding what he was after, Cinch appears in the doorway again and waves a small envelope in the air.

He looks at it, then pulls it close to his face and squints as if he's trying to read the name scribbled on the front. "Amelia and Spencer."

"That's us." She takes the envelope from his outstretched hand, looking at me first before tearing it open and reading it out loud.

My sweets,

If you're reading this, then you're with Cinch about to hop behind the wheel of the Dream Chaser. That's been her name as long as I've had her, and I'll leave it to you and Spencer to decide if that's the name she keeps.

I know this may seem like an odd request, but I need your help. Over the years, during my travels, I've left valuables here and there. I did a good job gathering them up before I ended up losing my driver's license, but there are a few places I didn't make it to—and this is where I need your help.

In this envelope, you'll find a map, directions, and some info to get you to your next location. If you are able to help me, your mission is to get to the Midnight Oasis RV Park in Ginnie Springs and find Big Andy.

Good luck, love you so,

Aunt Hattie

"That's it?" Putting the letter down, Amelia looks at me, her jaw slack. "Go to Ginnie Springs and ask for Big Andy?"

I take the letter from her hand and scan it, rereading the words she had read aloud a few moments prior. I'm as stumped as she is.

"You're gonna need supplies," Cinch's words are said slowly, drawn out so you can make out each syllable. He may sound a little like Forrest Gump, but he's right. We will need supplies.

"Is there a grocery store nearby?

"Sure is. There's a Publix over the bridge as you head out of Sarasota and get back to the highway." He swipes the map off the table and points to a spot that's been highlighted. "It's about three hours to Ginnie Springs by car, but since you're in an RV, you need to allow it to take longer."

"How long should it take us?" Amelia asks.

"Could take closer to three and a half or four hours, depending on traffic this time of year. Snowbirds like to come in from Canada."

Amelia and I exchange a look of confusion, which Cinch catches. "Snowbirds are what we call the people who come here to get away from their winter." He nods knowingly. "Just know you don't need to rush. Driving an RV is a lot different than driving a car."

Putting my sunglasses on, I peer over at Amelia. "Have you ever driven an RV?"

Judging from the look she shoots me, I'm guessing no. "I watched a few YouTube videos on the plane."

Beside me, Cinch snorts, which in turn makes Amelia's shoulders hike up next to her ears.

Looking at the size of the RV, and particularly its length, it's fair to say I'm questioning her abilities, but if I told her I was, she'd kill me. She can be independent, this one.

She crosses her arms and narrows her eyes as if reading my mind. "Are you doubting my driving skills?"

I quickly throw my hands up in mock surrender. "Not at all, it's just these things are different from driving a car."

She rolls her eyes. "Obviously."

"You know, I had to drive one for a movie I did one time. Maybe I should be the one to drive it for the first leg. At least to get us to the Midnight Oasis?"

"Let me get this straight." The amusement on her face doesn't get past me. "Because you drove one once, in a movie, you think you're okay to drive it now...for realsies?"

I'm going to ignore the sarcasm in her tone. "Please. Of course I can."

"You also played a doctor on TV once." She threads her arms in front of her. "Are you going to tell me that you can scrub in for surgery now, too?"

Taking a breath, I try not to laugh. She makes me nuts, but even I have to admit that she's funny.

"Look, I can tell you're tired, so why not let me drive and you can navigate the first part, okay?"

I can tell when Amelia's digging her heels in. Unthreading her arms, she puts her hands on her hips and looks at me, then back to the RV, to Cinch, and back to me one last time.

"Fine." She holds her hands up in front of her. "You drive. Barney and I'll do the navigating. But"—she wags a finger in my direction—"if I get anxious, we have to pull over."

I bow at the waist like a royal servant from days gone by. "Whatever m'lady needs."

"You two." If I'm not mistaken, Cinch guffaws at us as he rolls his eyes. "The Bickersons."

"The Bickersons?" Amelia snorts as she spins on her heel, tilting her head to one side to address Cinch. "What do you mean by that?"

"Hattie told me about the two of you. She told me if y'all rolled up here arguing amongst yourselves, I'm to tell you to shut your traps and work together. You can't fight and be in an RV, there's nowhere to hide. You've got to work together in an RV." He shakes his head and jerks a thumb over his shoulder toward his dwelling. "Let me grab the keys and we'll get the two of you on your way."

Cinch disappears from sight, rattling around in his camper again leaving us to stand quietly, with me thinking about what he just said.

He's right. We need to get along if we're going to make it back to Sweetkiss Creek in one piece. But how are we going to do that when we can barely go an hour without arguing? If one of us isn't poking the bear, the other is.

Amelia sighs, her head hanging low as she massages her temples.

Taking a few steps, I stand beside her and nudge her with my finger. "You good?"

"I'm fighting a headache, I'm hungry, and I'm really hoping we get back home before Christmas." Clenching her eyes closed, she slaps herself across the forehead, her breathing starting to come in stops and spurts. "And now I can't remember if I turned off the burner on the stove this morning."

I recognize this Amelia. Stressed Amelia whose anxiety could get the best of her. Her face pinches, and I slide my cell phone out of my back pocket and hand it to her.

"Here." I all but shove the phone into her hands. "Call

one of your friends and ask someone to go right now to your place to check."

Eyeing the phone, she hiccups as she calms her breathing. I know the signs of her small panic attacks when she's on the brink. She reaches out in what I think is an attempt to take the phone, but instead, she takes my hand and clutches it.

"Hey." I pull her close to me, the humidity causing my chest to go slick with sweat as soon as the heat of her body hits mine, and I don't care. "Just breathe. Like he said, we can't rush it."

Amelia snickers against my chest. "I think he was talking about the RV."

"Could be." Cracking a smile, I pet her hair, but as I go to kiss the top of her head, she steps away.

"Thanks." She runs her fingers through her hair before pulling it back and up, fastening it into a ponytail high on the top of her head. "Stinking panic attacks. That one came on fast."

I want to reach out and grab her, pull her back close to me and tell her how much I love her. But I can't. Not yet. Instead, I step back, giving her some space.

"You can always let me know when you need a minute." I squeeze her arm. "I'm right here."

Like Cinch said, there's no rush.

EIGHT

Amelia

If you've ever been treated to a wave of anxiety, followed by flashes of heat and warmth in your body, and then maybe a feeling of passing out or like you're going to faint, all while your heart is slamming loudly in your chest, then welcome to my world.

I've been in that state of flux for an hour before, but today I've managed to have two panic attacks within a few hours' time, and this trip is just starting. The first one on Siesta Key was over quickly. Spencer knows what to do, and he usually finds a way to calm me.

But this panic attack, the one I'm in the middle of right this very moment, is one he can't talk me off the ledge from. I can't lean into him for his strength or look to him for help because he's the one causing it.

"Look," Spencer says, his voice songlike as he flicks his right hand my way, pointing to a random home we're flying past with a lush front yard that's been decorated for the holidays. It's still daylight, so we're not going to be treated to seeing any Christmas lights on this leg of the trip, but that's fine with me. I just want to get where we're going and not be moving, or in this *thing* anymore, and the man does not realize when he points to the right, for some reason, this contraption lurches to the left.

"Please keep your eyes on the road," I snap with a hint of begging. Being on a wide-open highway with smooth roads is one thing, but when you get off the highway and are on side roads that clearly need some attention—and funding from the government—there is no room for mistakes.

"Sorry." Spencer shoots me one of his famous sideways smirks, flicking his hand in the air with an apologetic wave as he turns the radio up. He only raises the volume a smidge, but I can tell it's enough that he can drown me, and any of my complaints, out.

Looking down at my hands, I open my closed fists to look at where my fingernails have embedded themselves into the soft flesh of my palm. I'm positive the markings will be there forever, to remind me that Spencer cannot drive an RV for the life of him.

Who knew I'd compare riding in the front seat of this giant soup can with wheels to bungee jumping? Not that I've ever done that, nor do I have any plan to, but it's what I think it feels like. Like you're high in the air, looking at the moving pavement below and the scenes flitting past dirty windows, all while suspended over a canyon with no one or nothing to ground you.

I can't help my panic, it just is. I get to work through my anxiety when it flares up. It's safe to say this trip is kicking it right to the surface, and I'm willing to bet money that my hair will be falling out by nighttime.

Wanting to keep my mind off things, I scoop Barney into my arms and hold him while I busy myself staring out the windshield looking for our next turn. A cheer rises in my throat when a sign appears promising the turn to the Midnight Oasis is coming up. Before I can point it out,

Spencer has the blinker on and is slowing down, turning the RV carefully down a narrow dirt road.

Stifling my third yawn in the last ten minutes, I keep an eye on the road and another on Spencer as we approach a one-lane bridge. On the other side of it, at last, is our spot for the night.

The bridge crosses a small part of the river that forks off of the Santa Fe, crossing over a section of rapids. I'm mesmerized by the tumbling of the water over the rocks below as the sun begins its descent over the mountains to our left.

"Wow, this is gorgeous." Spencer's words are hushed, and he's right. Smiling his way, I offer him the gentle reminder I know he needs.

"Hey." Tapping on the dashboard three times, I snap my fingers and point to the road ahead. "Eyes on the road, please."

He may be smiling, but I notice how his jaw tightens. I know I'm irritating him, but this is a tiny need of mine, right now, to feel somewhat in control. If I don't trick my brain like this, I'll spin out.

We've been married for eight years. I know this man better than he knows himself, and I know how he can get distracted. The scenery is gorgeous in this part of Florida and my head won't stop swiveling on its axis, so I can only imagine how it's pulling his attention.

"Amelia," he manages through gritted teeth, somehow dragging my name out like a piece of taffy, twisty and sticky so it has three distinct syllables. Still smiling, though. "You don't have to keep telling me to watch the road."

"I don't want to have to say it, Spencer, but to be fair, you keep looking around while you're driving. This RV is new to us; it's not like you've been driving it for years."

"You're overthinking things," he chortles. Chortler. Mr. Big Poopy McChortlepants Ha-Ha from the fun-time factory.

I wag a finger in the air. "I'm just cautious."

"You know I like to throw caution to the wind," he teases. "It's not like you've ever driven one of these things yourself. Just sit there and relax; we're almost to the campground."

Even Barney eyes him warily as Spencer maneuvers the motorhome onto the narrow one-lane bridge. It's so narrow, it feels like we're putting on a corset. My heart pounds while I tick down an internal list of reasons why no campervan or RV of any kind should ever have to cross a bridge this tiny and rickety.

"Oh, look," Spencer says, once again tossing his right hand out to the side, pointing into the ether as far as I'm concerned. He almost smacks me in the chest in his rush to point out the pastel colors of the Florida sunset lingering on the river.

Seeing nature in all of her beauty makes me smile, and it touches me that Spencer wants to share this moment with me. My shoulders ease, the tension beginning to fade somewhat. It's been a long time since we shared anything with one another, and this? This is nice.

For a second, one moment in time, there is no worry, no pressure, and no stress. I let out the gulp of air I'd been holding on to since we drove onto the bridge and, smiling, look Spencer's way, ready to enjoy this moment with him, one anxious breath at a time.

When I look over, he's even more mesmerized than I am, staring beyond me and out the window. A bolt of icy panic rushes through me and an alarm in the back of my mind begins to go off.

My eyes flick to the steering wheel and, as if in slow motion, Spencer begins a monologue, rambling about the glorious view as he overcompensates with the steering wheel and pulls it left. At the same time, my hands fly to my mouth in an attempt to shove the scream that's coming out right back inside of me.

A sickening, screeching sound of metal grinding against

metal fills the air and pierces my ears. Shaking against my chest, Barney nuzzles his face into my hair as if trying to hide.

"Spencer!"

"What?"

If I'm not mistaken, the man is clueless. I jerk a thumb over my shoulder out the window. "You hit the bridge!"

"I did?" He gives me a look like I'm messing with him and shakes his head. "No, that was the bridge making that noise. It's old."

In a few moments, we're in the parking lot for the campground. Spencer pulls the RV into a parking space for registration. In an instant, I'm out of the RV first to see what the damage is.

"See?" I point to the front tire, where a hubcap used to be, as Spencer joins me. "I bet if we walk back to the bridge we'll find the hubcap there."

"Seriously?" He shakes his head, bewildered. Then, something on the back tire catches his eye as his cheeks flush bright red. "Oh, man. Looks like the back tire lost its hubcap, too."

"You said you could drive an RV, Spencer." Running my fingers through my hair, I fight the urge to scream again.

"They taught us how to drive one for that movie." He shakes his head. "I didn't have any problems then."

"Sometimes, you slay me, Spencer. Really. I'm sure you were driving in a safe area with plenty of people to look out for you and a stunt driver if you needed one." I hand him Barney's leash. "Here. Can you keep him safe while I go ask for Big Andy?"

He rolls his eyes, taking the leash. "Yes."

"Spencer Stoll. Can I trust you to wait here?"

"I think we can manage." He grins at Barney. "Cross those paws for luck, buddy."

Putting a hand on my hip, I point in his direction as he holds up a hand to show me his fingers are crossed.

I make sure to turn around so he doesn't see the smile I'm fighting because it won't stay hidden much longer. One of the reasons I fell in love with this man was the fact that no matter what, even in the middle of full-out panic, he can make me laugh.

Flinging the door open to reception, I'm surprised when I walk in to find myself at the back of a small line. Granted there's only two people ahead of me, one currently chatting away with an older woman whose long silver hair is piled high into a bun on top of her head—but still. It's Christmas at an RV park, are there really any other people who are going to be here?

Dragging my eyes around the room, I notice each wall has a purpose in the small lobby. One wall houses a community bulletin board, complete with notices on it for folks who may want a babysitter or items for sale, mostly camping gear. Another wall boasts a map of the area showing all of the trails and outdoor activities nearby. A third wall is covered in photos; some of them are faded to brown and sepia colors telling me they've been hanging on the wall for a long time.

I let my eyes wander over the photos, taking in the groups of smiling happy people in the pictures. Snapshots from years gone by showing families at their campsites setting up their tents, photos shared of groups going tubing on the river in the summertime, and there's a cluster of photos in the corner of several people standing in the middle of a small clearing with a familiar RV in the background.

I check my place in line, making sure no one's coming in behind me because I don't want to lose my spot, and I step closer to inspect this particular photo. There's something about one of the women in the picture that I can't put my finger on until I get right up on top of it.

My heart skips a little beat as I tap my finger on the photo. Aunt Hattie. We're definitely in the right place.

"Welcome to the Midnight Oasis," someone sings out, startling me so I jump a hair. "Can I help you?"

My head snaps to attention, and the beautiful bohemian woman behind the front counter smiles.

With one last look at the picture, I step up to the counter. "I hope so. I'm looking for two things. One, we'd love to stay the night if you have the space, and two, I need to find someone named Big Andy. I think he lives here or nearby?"

"Well, I can help with both." I didn't think this woman's grin could get any wider, but it does. She's such a tiny thing, like a fairy. All she needs are some wings and a little more sparkle, and she'll be set. "I'm Andrea, but my really close friends call me Big Andy, and there's not many of them left these days."

"I'm Amelia." I turn back and point to the photograph on the wall. "Believe it or not, but my aunt sent me to see you."

"Of course she did," she says, her expression softening more. There's sadness reflected in her eyes. "Oh, I miss her. She was the best." She treats me to one last grin as she bends down and disappears from sight behind the counter, springing up a moment later with a small envelope in her hand. "She gave this to me earlier this year. It's for you. I was told to instruct you to read it later."

I recognize the writing on the front. Another note from Aunt Hattie. Grinning, I hold it close to my heart. Gotta admit, this is kind of cool. "Thank you."

"That's not all," she says as she opens a drawer and pulls out a map. She points to a spot not far from a building labeled the activities center. "You need a space to stay and we can provide it. I've got a spot for you with an electric hookup. You'll be able to use the power in your motorhome and turn the heat on, which is good because it can get chilly at night."

"That's good to know. The RV is new to me; I'm not scared to admit that we're learning as we go." Stifling a yawn,

I take the map from her and tuck it into my back pocket. I can already tell I'll be sleeping really well tonight. Like, I'm gonna be snoring kind of sleep. Probably drool, too. "Thanks again."

"Wait, I almost forgot. She also asked me to make sure I give you this." Turning around, she opens a cabinet door and pulls out a cardboard box. "She said that when you get it, I'm supposed to tell you not to open this until she tells you to."

Talk about a Christmas miracle. "How is she going to—"

"One thing I know about your aunt," Andy says with a laugh, "is that she would have had her reasons for why." She shrugs a shoulder and winks. "Just go with it. One of my favorite quotes, and one of your aunt's, too, is from the Rev. Dr. Martin Luther King: 'You don't have to see the whole staircase, just take the first step.'" She leans over the counter and squeezes my hand, pale green eyes blinking back tears. "This, my dear, could be your first step—a reason to have faith."

The tinkling of the bell over the door interrupts my thoughts as Andy looks past me to greet the newcomer. Mumbling my thanks, I gather my things and am halfway out the door when she calls out to me.

"By the way, did anyone explain the toilet and how to work the cassette to you?"

I rack my brain trying to think of anything that looks like a cassette player that would be in the toilet of the RV. "Like a cassette tape?"

Andy and the man at the counter exchange a chortle. If I had to name it, I'd call it a chortle of experience. "No, not like a tape. Like the thing you do your 'ones' and 'twos' in."

My stomach dips with a sick anticipation. They can't mean what I think they do. "What do you mean by 'ones' and 'twos?'"

"When you have to go to the bathroom," Andy giggles.

"You have to empty the toilet cassette. No one explained this to you?"

How is it that I own a campground and I've never heard of this until now? It could be because we don't host RVs, but now that I have one that may need to change. Yet another part of this RV life I hadn't taken into consideration. "So the cassette is part of the toilet in the RV?"

Andy's head bobs up and down. "Watch some videos on YouTube before you go and let me know if you have any questions."

Ignoring their cackling laughter, I square my shoulders, open the door, and walk out with my head held high.

I've taught myself how to do a lot of things in this life. I taught myself French. When I wanted to learn how to knit, I sat down with a YouTube video and learned that. I'm not a DIY queen, but I can avoid a Pinterest fail.

Anyone can learn anything from YouTube. You can learn to build a house on YouTube if you want...surely I can learn how to clean the toilet, too.

"We have to empty...that." Biting down on my lip, I fight the dry retch forming at the back of my throat. Andy was right in advising me to watch these videos, I mean...who knew?

Spencer, who's been sitting beside me at the tiny kitchen table watching along with me, shakes his head as he puts his hand in the air. "Not it."

"You don't get to cop out, Spencer." I nudge him with my elbow. "I need you to step up and learn how to empty the cassette. You know RVs, remember?"

He pinches his eyes closed tight and shakes his head from side to side. "I really don't want to talk about this anymore."

"And you think I do?" Shuddering, I close my laptop and

lean back against the high back of the booth. "This is made of nightmares. Thank goodness the Midnight Oasis has toilets and a shower we can use so we don't have to use the ones in here."

Turning in his seat, Spencer looks toward the back of the motorhome at the accordion door which doubles as the entrance for the shower behind me. Across from that, there's a door that leads into a space the size of a closet, and that's where the toilet is.

The RV is well planned out—even if it isn't what I'd call spacious, there's still plenty of room for us to move around. The bedroom is beyond the shower and is currently set up as two single twin beds with three steps in between them, good to use if you need a boost to get into bed or so you can reach the storage at the end of the RV, above where one lays their head.

Before we left Siesta Key, Cinch had shown us how the two single beds can be made into one king-size bed. It's as simple as sliding a piece of wood, which will act as the base, over the gap where the steps are. Once that's in place, you can add a small section of mattress, which is kept in the rear storage space, to the middle part. And voila: king bed, lots of room, party time.

"Fine." When I look over at Spencer, he winks. "It can't be that hard to change the toilet cassette; I'm sure I can do it."

"Okaaaay," I say, drawing the word out as I fight the smirk dancing on my lips.

"Anyway, we don't have to worry about it right this minute," he presses on, ignoring me. "We can use the shower in here. Cinch told us he filled up the water."

I'm not convinced. "I'll be using the facilities, thank you."

"Whatever." Spencer takes the laptop, sliding it in front of him and opens it again, pulling up more videos. "I'm going to watch some more videos about this. Did you know that the whole back of this thing is nothing but storage? I bet we could fit a refrigerator for our house in that empty space."

"It's an RV, not a mansion." I stifle another yawn, throwing my hands overhead and stretching, careful not to take out the curtains hanging beside me. This is when I notice the button on the wall next to me. "What's that do?"

Not even taking a second to consider what he's about to do, Spencer reaches across me, winking, and taps it. As soon as he pulls away, the sound of an engine cranking to life fills the air around us. A sound comes from above, and when I crane my neck to see where it's coming from, the ceiling begins moving and presses down on top of me.

"Spencer!" My panic is feral, but who wouldn't be if they were stuck in the back corner of a booth literally with the walls of a motorhome closing in around them? Out of sheer terror, and probably some reflex, I smack the button hoping to make it stop. My attention snaps back to watch for a sign that the ceiling is slowing down or, for the love of Santa, stopping, and luckily it does.

Holding my heart, I look at Spencer, who's grinning. Leaning back across me, he taps the button again and the ceiling begins rising and going back into place.

"Well," he manages as a chuckle stutters its way out, "looks like I found the second bed."

Hearing the word bed, I yawn yet again. Exhaustion is sinking in and, judging by the look Barney's shooting in my direction, he wants a walk before bed, so I need to rally. My eyes close on their own, willing me to lie down. But I can feel Spencer's eyes on me, watching me. Knowing this sends a ribbon of heat pulsing through my insides.

I've spent the last year either being sad or mad, and I think I'm getting to that point where I've come full circle in my frustration. I've wanted for so long for us to be able to talk, to be in the same room so we could work on us. Now I have the time, and everything feels more electric than it did only days ago. Like every moment counts and in ways it hasn't before.

"So." Spencer clears his throat. "Are you going to open the envelope?"

Opening my eyes, I shake my head. "Barney needs a walk first, and then we should eat."

"I think I saw a grill." Spencer hops up and opens one of the cabinets where I shoved some of our groceries. He holds up the hamburger buns and ketchup. "How about if I throw some burgers on for us after I get a shower?"

The rumble in my stomach tells me it's the best idea ever. "That sounds great. Thank you."

"And I'm going to try our shower here." He indicates with his head to the back of the motorhome. "Are our suitcases back there?"

Nodding, I slide out of the booth behind him and grab Barney's leash, clipping it to his collar. "Whatever floats your boat. I brought towels. They're back there, too, if you need one."

Twinkling blue eyes anchor my gaze to his. "You always think of everything. Thanks."

There's something in his voice that causes my heart to hitch. Holding his attention, I keep my eyes centered on his— have they always been this blue? There's an icy coolness to them, with flecks of sunlit currents swirling. A shudder works its way up my spine, and my traitorous heart slams so hard inside my chest, I'm fairly certain he can hear it.

Needing to put some space between us here, I open the door and Barney flies out, sniffing the grass and smelling all the smells around our campsite. Hopping down the steps behind him, I turn back around to tell him he's welcome, only now Spencer is standing before me...in all of his shirtless glory.

Legs like Jell-O? Tick. I try to keep my eyes focused from the neck up, but they keep finding their way down, the sculpted 'V' of his lower abs all but glistens. This man has been working out, and it shows in every glorious ripple.

"Medium rare?" Spencer asks.

"What?" Like I can think about anything other than those abs right now.

"I asked if you want your burger medium rare." Pulling a slow smile, he treats me to a crinkle of a grin. The enjoyment dancing across his face as I sway listlessly in my satiated discomfort is too much. "That's still your go-to temperature, right?"

"Oh, yeah." I'd love to take my temperature right now. I'm sure it's off the charts. "Thanks."

Spinning around quickly, I start jogging away with Barney trying to keep up for dear life. There's so much we still need to discuss that hasn't come up, and I don't even know how to broach the topic of us anymore.

But for now, I can enjoy the eye candy.

NINE

Spencer

Morning comes faster than I thought it would. I swear I'd only just gotten my head on the pillow when I was awakened by the sounds of the campervan beside us as they packed up their things and left, hitting the road for their next journey.

Rolling over in my perch from the bed above the dining area, I can see that Amelia is still fast asleep with Barney snuggled beside her. All I want to do is slide out of my bed and climb in beside her and kiss her good morning, tell her I'm sorry over and over, and try this whole thing again. The Amelia of days gone by would be open to my silliness, welcoming. In fact, she'd encourage it.

This Amelia asked me to sleep in the second bed last night, even though I fell asleep—accidentally on purpose—on her bed. This Amelia is a little bit testier, and I can't blame her. I need to own up to my part in this relationship if we're going to get it right.

There's a soft groan as Amelia rolls over and pulls Barney closer to her body. I watch as her eyes flutter open, taking in her quarters before they lock into mine.

She narrows her eyes. "Are you staring at me?"

"Kinda." Do I admit I have been for at least an hour? "I'm willing you the power to drive today."

"You said you wanted to do it," she manages to say sassily around a yawn.

"But I don't want to drive it the whole way back. You're going to have to do some of the driving, too, you know."

"Of course, I know." Scowling, she sits up as Barney stretches his body from the very tip of his front paws to his tail, opening his eyes for only a brief moment before closing them again and drifting back to puppy dreamland. I bet it's peaceful there. "I'm going to drive—I'm more than capable. In fact, I'll take the first leg."

Defensive Amelia is back. "I didn't mean you had to do it now."

"Honestly, Spencer, let me do it." She pulls her hair back into a low ponytail. "I feel like if I drive, we'll get there with the RV still in one piece."

Ouch. "It was just the hubcaps."

"This time," Amelia says as she throws her arms in the air above her and gives her own upper body a thorough stretch, treating me to a view of her curves. Curves I know like the back of my own hand, but ones that now feel unfamiliar like when you move away from home and come back only to find that some old building you used to love has been torn down. Replaced by something newer, sharper, maybe with cleaner lines.

She points to what looks like a couple of dented silver platters on the floor by her bed. "Do you know what those are?"

Squinting my eyes, I prop myself up on an elbow, leaning forward to get a better view. Upon further inspection, what was thought to be a couple of old trays turns out to be—*the* hubcaps. Chewing on the inside of my cheek, I drag my eyes to meet hers, slowly, and nod my head once. Because once is enough.

She holds her hands in the air. "Now you see why I'm worried."

"You can trust me with the RV, Amelia."

"It's not just the RV, Spencer," she says, flipping her hair. "It's all the other things that go with it."

I knew it. "So, it's about not trusting me?"

"I didn't say that." She holds a finger up and shakes it at me. "Not my words. At all."

"You didn't have to say it, it's implied."

They say silence is golden, but not when it hangs in the air like a humid thunderstorm on a hot August afternoon. Not that it's August or afternoon, but still.

Huffing, Amelia tosses the top sheet off her body and throws her legs over the side of the bed, her toes tapping as they hit the floor. She disappears into the toilet only to return a few moments later fully dressed and holding the map.

I'm impressed by her speed and abilities. It's a small room. Perfect for a couple of Keebler elves, and a toilet, but that's about all. "That was fast."

"I laid my clothes out last night after I opened the envelope and looked the map over."

Seeing the torn envelope clutched in her hand, I can admit I'm hurt. "You opened the envelope without me?"

"You were passed out and snoring." She picks it up from where it's lying on the bed beside her. "There wasn't a note in this one, just a map and a name for our next location."

"Oh." I'm still feeling some unknown feelings here. "What's it say?"

"We're looking for a man named Gerry at Stone Mountain Park. It's just outside of Atlanta." She sits back down on her bed and opens the map up, her finger trailing a line. "The roads are open highway, and there's no construction from what I could see when I looked the route up online last night. Should take us about four or five hours. Tops."

"Where was I when you were out getting the hubcaps, laying out clothes, and planning our drive today?"

"I told you." She inclines her head in Barney's direction. "Both of you were passed out and I couldn't sleep, so I planned."

Of course she did. Ask me to point out something I love about this woman and being organized would have to be at the top of the list, if not in the top ten for sure. Right behind the sexy smile, infectious laugh, and the best kisses I've ever had, that is.

Aching to be next to her, I get up under the guise of "looking at the route" and sit beside her, putting my chin on her shoulder. A thrill shoots through my body like electric heat when she doesn't pull away or shrug me off.

"So this route," I ask, leaning into her body with mine, pressing up against her as I angle my mouth closer to her ear, "this is the one we want to take?"

Her breath hitches, but she still doesn't move. "Um, yes."

I want to see how far I can take this. Angling my nose so it's nestled in her hair, I snake an arm around her waist and, using my other, point to another part of the highway. This time I move my mouth so my lips are closer to a spot I know well. Really well. It's her sweet spot, located right behind her earlobe.

"What if we took a detour and went on this road...here?" Using the last word as a kind of crutch, I breathe out, letting the heat of my breath hit her skin. I can feel the prickling of goosebumps on her flesh as I slide my fingers up her forearm. Her body is pressed into mine as she turns toward me. Slowly at first, stopping to lick her beautiful, full, pink lips as her hand flies out instinctively to grasp mine.

Bowing my head to be even closer still, I close my eyes and

pull her to me. Only, this time, Amelia stiffens. In what feels like a millisecond, she's up and away, clearing her throat and pointing outside.

"I should go tell Andy goodbye. Can you move your bed for me?" She taps on its frame. "So cool that it lowers from the ceiling, but it's in the perfect spot so I can't get out."

In a matter of mere moments, she's up and out, running away from me and what I know was a moment where she felt something, too.

Grinning to myself, I grab clothes to throw on for the day.

There's no rush.

It'll only take about four hours, she said. Four hours, maybe five tops. Give or take.

Make it six hours, two bathroom breaks, and one argument later, and you'll have the amount of time it takes to get from Ginnie Springs Florida to "just outside of Atlanta."

"You should have stopped and asked for directions, you know." My tone comes out with a touch more bite than intended, evidenced by Amelia's lip twitch.

She gives me a serving of side-eye. "You should zip that lip before I reach across the cab and zip it for you."

"You're being a bit aggressive, 'Melia."

I'm rewarded with a half-grin when I bust out her nickname. "I really don't feel like I'm being aggressive. Laying a boundary, yes, aggressive, no."

"Passive-aggressive?" I query.

"I really don't want to hear any more about it, Spencer. I swear to all things that...oh, yes! Look!" She points excitedly to a sign ahead. "Stone Mountain, next exit."

"I can't wait for you to stop this thing." Punching my

hands in the air, I put my feet on the dashboard and let out a whoop of joy. "I. Am. Tired."

"Oh, please," she cackles. "You only drove for like a half-hour on that last leg before I took over. We both know I've pulled the hard miles on my own."

It's like there's something in the sentence that gives me dead-man-walking vibes all of a sudden. Like she's laying down a gauntlet related to our relationship in the form of a road trip.

Kicker is, she's not *that* wrong.

"I know you did," I acknowledge. And, even though I want to, of course I'm not going to point out her mistake: that when she took over driving for me, she'd taken the incorrect highway and we'd driven for at least forty-five minutes in the wrong direction before we realized what she'd done. I don't want to bicker.

"Hey," Amelia says, getting my attention, pointing to a spot in the distance. "Over there, are those fireworks?"

Following where she points, I see sparkling lights as they go off, popping overhead in the evening sky. My attention is then drawn to a digital billboard on the side of the highway.

I point to it. "Looks like the Stone Mountain Christmas Parade is happening today."

The sign flashes, warning us and other drivers of a backup on the highway ahead. As Amelia turns on the blinker to signal us exiting the highway, I'm reminded it's something we luckily don't have to worry about. At least not this time. It's like the universe looked down on us and felt we'd been handed enough lumps of coal for one day, so why not give us some sugary treats instead?

At the end of the exit ramp, we're greeted by signage telling us to go left across the bridge for four miles until we come to the campground. Pulling up outside the main gate, we both spot a sign posted asking visitors and guests to ring the doorbell upon arrival. I jump out and ring the buzzer, and stand waiting for a response when two girls sidle up next to me. Out of the corner of my eye, I see them put their heads close together, one of them trying to subtly point at me but yet not really point, more of a motioning of her hand. Something I notice because it's just me, two strangers, and a gate.

We all stand awkwardly, one of the girls now staring intently at her cell phone while the other keeps an eye on me. Shivering in the cooler night air, I tap the buzzer again. This time, there's some success and a sign of life as the box buzzes to life.

"Welcome to Stone Mountain RV Park, can I help you?"

"Uh, yeah," I say leaning into the voice box with an eye on the two girls, who are both now fiddling with their cell phones. I turn around so my back faces them and press my lips close to the speaker. "I have a reservation under..." I look at the paper to see what name we're registered under and shake my head. "Hattie the fabulous."

The girls giggle while the speaker box stays silent. We stand there for a second, with me contemplating if I should ring the buzzer again. Luckily I don't have to think about it for too long. The grinding of metal and whirring of a small motor coming to life signals the gate is opening. Thrilled we're almost inside to the part where we get to eat dinner and get some sleep, I almost skip back to the RV.

When I climb back inside with Amelia, though, there's a shift in the air and energy, as if a cold front has moved in.

"I think those girls figured out who you are," she says, clicking her tongue on the roof of her mouth.

I shrug. "It's fine. I'm sure they'll leave us alone."

Amelia throws the RV into drive and begins to pull forward slowly, her eyes staying trained on her driver's-side mirror, watching the two girls.

"I don't know, Spencer, you know me and my gut."

I do and it's usually spot on. "You got a feeling?"

She looks at me sheepishly. "Maybe we should tell the campsite manager about them, just to be safe."

I appreciate when she gets like this, but it's overkill. "I'm fine."

Shaking her head, she pulls up beside the office door and throws the RV into park. Reaching across me, she grabs the baseball hat out of the center console and tosses it to me. "Fine. If you're fine, I'm fine, but I need you to wear this, please."

When my eyes meet hers, they flicker with worry and caution. She's always been careful to keep our private life private, and I've always worked hard with her to respect that. I know better than to say no when she's in protective mode, so I slide it on my head and open my door.

Ducking into the office, we both head straight to the small woodstove to warm ourselves. The reception area is small but cozy, with a couch and two small chairs on one side of the room. On the other side is a long shelf against the wall lined with a giant platter of Christmas cookies, a variety of teas, and urns—one I assume for coffee and the other, most likely full of hot water for tea.

Amelia digs into the snacks, helping herself to a donut while she pours herself a cup of coffee. Me, I'm watching her and once again fighting the urge to pull her into my arms and smother her with kisses.

"Can I help you?"

Turning around to greet the person attached to the voice, I'm pleased to see he's wearing a name tag, and it says *Gerry.*

"You certainly can," I say, pointing to his name tag. "We're looking for you."

"Don't I know you?" As the older man leans forward on his hands, sizing me up, I hear the bell on the front door tinkle, signaling more people have walked into the small reception area. "I do. You're that actor, aren't ya?"

Aware of my surroundings, I pull the hat down further over my eyes. "People tell me I look like that guy all the time."

The man keeps staring, hard-core now, while I wait for Amelia to bail me out. It's what she usually does, only she's not doing it now. When I turn around to see where my backup is, she's on the other side of the room eating another donut and talking to someone on her phone. Great.

"No." Gerry shakes his head, narrowing his eyes as he sizes me up. "It's your voice. It sounds like that guy."

Chuckling, I shrug a shoulder. "I'm just me."

The older man squints his eyes and, with one last look of what I take as disapproval now, he turns back to his guest register. "Do you have a reservation?"

My mouth barely opens with the word yes forming on my lips when I hear Amelia say goodbye to whoever she's talking to and call out to me. "We checked in now, Spencer?"

From behind me, I hear giggling. Spinning on my heel, I'm not surprised to find the same two girls from the front gate now standing inside with us, eyes wide, watching my movements. Amelia's face registers surprise, realization washing over her that she's outed me accidentally, as she clocks them as well.

"Wait, so you are Spencer Stoll." The man looks at me again, this time differently. "You're *the* Spencer Stoll, aren't ya?"

"Last I knew, yes," I chuckle.

"That means you're here with your wife. Amelia." He looks where Amelia stands beside the stove. "You're Hattie's niece. I've seen pictures of you."

"She told us to come here to find you," Amelia offers, taking a few steps to cross the room to stand beside me. "Well, not so much told us as left me instructions to come."

"Hattie was a rascal. This world is a lot quieter without her and her singing in it. She loved her karaoke." Kind eyes bounce from Amelia, to me, and back again. "So she sent you to me, huh?"

"She did." Amelia nods. "Said we'd need to ask for you and there might be something here I'm supposed to get from you?"

He tosses his head back, laughing. "She had me store a large suitcase here for her, left that stinking suitcase with me about six months ago. She told me you'd come for it eventually." He waves his hand at us. "And here you are."

Amelia does a small curtsy. "Here we are."

"Well, seeing as you have the *Dream Chaser*, I'll put you in Hattie's favorite spot at the back of the lot." He takes out a small map with the layout of the park, highlighting where we want to go. "It's got power and should be quiet now that the fireworks are over."

I take the map as he slides it across the counter to us. "Yeah, we noticed some fireworks when we were coming in. There's a Christmas Parade, too?"

"There was. It's actually our Founders Day weekend, but it coincides with our Christmas celebrations, so it is a little busy around here for wintertime. Just can't have any emergencies because things like needing a tow truck won't happen until morning, if at all."

"Is Founders Day kind of like a holiday around here?" Amelia asks.

Gerry grins. "Stone Mountain loves a party, and we love to shut down for them, too. It's mostly the people who fix things, like mechanics, locksmiths, plumbers, and all that...they like to take the day off and sometimes the day after. That's why we say 'no emergencies.'" He nods, his eyes flicking to the two girls dallying at the front door. "Why don't you go on and get settled and I'll bring the suitcase out to you in a little bit?"

It doesn't take us long to get to our spot, and we're both surprised by how many people are here. Judging by the rumble of my stomach and Amelia's, we're both in need of a meal.

"Hungry?"

"Starving." She looks out the window. "I'm ready for bed, but I can't stop worrying about those two girls. All it takes is for someone to get wind you're around here, and the paparazzi will pop up out of nowhere."

"I'm telling you, we're in the middle of nowhere Georgia and on our way to who-knows-where-ville. I doubt anyone cares that an actor, especially me, is in the vicinity." I don't care what she says, she overthinks. Two girls seeing me at a campground isn't enough for me to start worrying and call for help. "How about this: I'll start dinner. I can make us spaghetti— it's easy enough to whip up on that stove—and you can take Barney for a walk and clear your head."

"You know, that sounds awesome." She looks out the window again, pointing to the bathroom sign. "Let me run over there real quick and I'll come back for Barney."

I watch as she jogs away, smiling to myself. Spaghetti is one of her favorite meals. She likes it better when I take the time to make the pasta fresh, but I think she'll forgive me this once.

In a matter of minutes, I've got everything going: water is boiling for noodles, tomato sauce is heating up, the oven is on, and I'm about to toss garlic bread in. Grabbing my phone, I scroll through until I find a music app I want and the playlist I'm looking for. Tapping play, I get up and start moving around the RV, setting the table for dinner and entertaining Barney.

The steam from the noodles and the sauce adds to the heat of the small space, making it humid in no time. Feeling the heat, I pull my shirt off over my head and crack open a skylight above the kitchen. It's really beginning to feel sticky in here, so I move to crack a window over the small sink. Flinging open the curtains, I jump, startled to find the two girls from reception trying to peek inside.

Not even thinking, I open the door and go outside. In my rational thoughts, I'm thinking if I plead with them to leave us alone, kindly and gently, they will. I hurry my way around the side of the motorhome to where they were loitering, but by the time I get there, they're gone.

The cold air hits my skin, reminding me I'm half-naked out here. Shaking my head, I pull my shirt back on and make my way back around to the door. Grasping the small handle, I tug on it, but nothing happens.

Not sure what's going on, I pull on the handle again. And again. And one more time for good measure. It's not opening.

I hear footsteps walking up behind me. Prepared to turn around and see the two girls again, I plaster on my nicest smile only to have it fade when I find Amelia.

She looks at me quizzically. "What are you doing?"

"I locked the door by accident." I put my hand out expectantly. "Can I have the keys?"

Her eyes widen as she shakes her head. "I don't have them."

"What do you mean?" A cold blast of fear flows through my veins. "Where's the spare?"

"We weren't given one." Her eyes narrow. "Why are the windows steaming up?"

That blast of fear is now a firehouse of freaking out. "I'm in the middle of making dinner, Amelia."

"Where's Barney?" she asks, her voice cracking.

I swallow the lump in my throat. "Inside."

"So, you've got the stove on, left the dog inside, and we're locked out?"

I see where she's going with this.

TEN

Amelia

I am a woman who will always look for the solution instead of mulling over the problem. I've always been that way; action solves things faster than being stalled. Activation Amelia, that's what an old boss of mine used to call me when I worked for one of the film studios making acquisitions.

Thinking fast, I grab my phone, ready to search for a local locksmith who can help, but Spencer grabs my arm and stops me.

"Gerry just told us no one is available because of the Christmas Parade and Founders Day celebrations."

As if he needed to weigh in, a muffled but familiar *york!* comes from inside the motorhome. I know my dog's barks—he has a special one for going to the dog park (it's very excited, usually some happy howling involved) and then he's got another one for going to the vet (not as excited, more melancholy and tinged with worry). This one is the one tinged with worry, signaling his nervousness, which feeds into mine.

"We need to get in that RV, Spencer." Looking at him, I fold my arms in front of me in an effort to keep from pulling my hair out and screaming. "How did you leave the keys inside?"

"Why did you leave me with the keys?" he retorts.

"You're an adult, I figured you could handle it." Seeing the hurt flash across his face, I pull my tone in a bit, softening some, but still wanting to get my point across. "You left Barney in there. With fire going."

Spencer twists his hands together. "It's not fire. More like electricity that if we have to turn off we will and we can...we'll just unplug it from the source out here."

Okay, fine, he saved one aspect of this horror show. "That doesn't help us with the fact that we're out here and not in there."

Chomping at the literal bit, and shivering from the chill in the air, I walk around the RV for a few minutes in silence, looking for anything that may help me break into it and attempting to formulate a plan. Stepping away, I cast my eyes across the roof, craning my neck when something catches my eye. "Wait. You left the sunroof open."

"Huh?" Spencer is by my side in a few steps and looking up at the roof with me, his eyes landing on the open hatch. "Great. Something else for you to give me grief over."

"No, Spencer, and let's unpack that later, please." I point to the top of the motorhome, a low buzz building in my tummy. "The sunroof being open is a good thing. I think I can fit through it."

Spencer gives me a sideways look, which I try to ignore. "You sure you can get through that thing?"

Putting one hand on my hip, I swivel around and give him my best "no, you didn't say that" expression. "Are you saying I can't?"

"Nooo," he says, throwing his hands in front of him for protection. "I'm simply wondering if that sunroof may be a little more narrow than you think it is."

Motioning for him to follow me, I walk to the back of the RV where the bike rack is secured. "If you hoist me up, I'll use the rack to pull myself up and over, then I can climb onto the roof."

Rolling his eyes, Spencer does as he's told, crouching over and threading his fingers together to make a kind of stirrup out of his hands for me to put my foot in. Placing my hands on his shoulders, I slide my right foot onto his hands and bounce just a touch as he lifts me easily upward so I can grab the rack. Within seconds, I've pulled my body onto the top of the RV and am looking back down at Spencer and grinning.

I scramble—albeit slowly because I don't want the roof to collapse—across the length of the motorhome to the open sunroof. When I reach it, I peek inside and find the perfect view of the kitchen counter and Barney, who stares at me with a mix of excitement and confusion, probably thinking in his doggie mind that this is the best game ever.

Throwing one leg over the side of the hatch and then the other, being careful as to balance my weight on my forearms, I lower myself through the open hole gleefully.

I clear it with room to spare, my feet first touching the counter where I am able to get my balance under control to enter the RV. Once I'm there all the way in, it's two quick hops before landing on the floor beside a very happy dog.

Sitting beside Barney and scratching his head, I spy the stray keys on the counter by the stove. I shove them in my front pocket, then open the door, allowing one sheepish Spencer Stoll re-entry.

***

"You locked yourself out of this contraption?"

Gerry and his missing front tooth can't stop laughing at us. Normally, I'd be irritated, but tonight, I'm laughing with

Gerry. I'm full of gratitude: I'm glad we're in the RV because it's cold out there, I'm thankful for the food Spencer made us that did not burn on the stove, and I'm even grateful for Gerry and his laughter.

"Well, you've got Hattie's suitcase now," he says, shifting his weight from one foot to the other and pointing to the suitcase I chucked onto my bed in the back. "And I'm gonna suggest you go to a hardware store to get a spare key made at your next stop."

Spencer, who is parked with the driver's seat turned around a full one-eighty to face us, bounces his eyes from mine to Gerry's and back. "We definitely need an extra key made."

"True, however, I have a question." Leaning against the booth, I put one hand on the small dining table and tap my fingers slowly before looking up at Gerry, who stands stock-still in our doorway looking a little like Hagrid from Harry Potter, only slighter. "You said our 'next stop.' Do you know what it is we're doing?"

"Hattie came here to organize this little scavenger hunt for you two about a year ago." His grin fades, but his eyes glint with love and memories. "That was when she found out she wasn't going to be around for this year's Christmas."

"You must have been special to her if she was here so close to the holidays," Spencer acknowledges.

Gerry nods. "Hattie and I were together for a very long time."

Seeing the sadness in his eyes, I reach out and squeeze his arm. "You were in a relationship with my aunt?"

Hagrid, I mean Gerry, nods as he thumbs his beard. "She meant the world to me. I loved her. I was *in* love with her for years. That woman could do no wrong—she was always there for me, and I did my best to be there for her, no matter what."

A knock at our door stops Gerry mid-story. "Hope you

don't mind I told my son I'd be here. He's the only one watching the front desk."

We both motion for him to go ahead. He calls out for his son to come in, but before the door opens, he looks our way. "Just ignore the hair."

Spencer and I look at each other and shrug as the door opens. A young guy, probably in his teens, stands in front of us rocking a great tan and a bleached-blond short haircut. He says hello and turns his back to us to ask Gerry a question. As he does, my eyes rock over to find Spencer's eyes wide while staring at the kid's head. Rolling my eyes, I reach across the small table to smack his arm. He's so rude. I make a mental note to give him more grief when we're alone.

Using his head to indicate, Spencer points toward Gerry's son. When I look at the young man again, this time I can't help but stare as well. What looks like orange letters are stamped into the back of his hair, like a football field that's had paint sprayed on it. Rubbing my eyes, I look again, thinking it's the light, but no. It truly looks like this kid has somehow put orange lettering on his hair, only I don't think it spells anything, and if it does, it's not a word I've seen before.

Gerry's son turns and says goodbye, the door closing behind him. Gerry leans against the fridge and sighs. "I told that kid not to bleach his hair."

"You know it looks good," I say, finding the positive.

"Except for the Home Depot logo he's got now." Gerry chuckles. "That ding-dong used an old bag from there to cover his head when he was bleachin' it. That's why he's got 'Home Depot' spelled backward on his head, in case you were wondering."

My hand flies to my mouth, but it's too late. Spencer and I both start cracking up at the same time, but thankfully Gerry does, too. Once we've got that out of our systems, Spencer's the one who tries to get us back on track.

"So, you were talking about Aunt Hattie...what happened?" Spencer asks.

"I made promises to her about slowing down, that I wasn't going to keep working. I told her I'd step back and enjoy life with her." Gerry smiles, but his eyes are dark now with only what I can assume is remorse. "But I messed up and didn't do what I said I would. And your aunt was a proud woman, so she moved on in her own way."

My eyes don't have to travel far to find Spencer's—we lock in one another, exchanging a knowing look. Fighting the lump in my throat, I wonder if the same thing floating through my mind is going through his. I swallow the lump down and turn back toward Gerry.

"Anyway..." Gerry steps forward and puts an envelope on the table, sliding it toward me. "This is your next mission, should you choose to accept it," he finishes with a wink.

Not one to wait, I tear the envelope open and pull out a map and a small piece of paper scribbled with instructions.

"Oh," Gerry interrupts. "I'm also supposed to tell you not to open the suitcase until it's time."

"Until it's time?" I have no idea what he means.

Gerry shrugs. "She said you'll know when you know."

Standing up, Spencer reaches over and takes one of the papers from my hands, scanning his eyes across it. "So we're headed to Fountain Creek, South Carolina. A place called Ramblin' Rick's RV Park."

"Used to be Ramblin' Rose's, but when she and Rick split, he kept it," Gerry muses thoughtfully, snapping his gum.

"So, I guess we're off first thing tomorrow, then." I stifle a yawn, my weary body about to break. "There's a note here it takes around three hours to drive there, so in an RV, I'm thinking it's going to take longer."

Spencer nods. "We need to stop for gas, too."

"And a key." I wag my finger in the air. "We can't forget that."

"Okay, you two," Gerry says. "I'll leave you to get your rest. Stop in to say 'bye before you go."

He's almost out the door when he turns around and looks at me, pointing. "When I last saw Hattie, we spoke about how we ended up. She had forgiven me, but I wasn't able to forgive myself and don't think I'll ever be able to."

Gerry's eyes find their way to Spencer and then back to mine. "You're so much like her. You know, she would talk about you." He looks at me with what I can only compare to wisdom flashing in his eyes. "Both of you. And she was worried that you two would end up like we did. So, if you haven't had a 'sign,' as she liked to call them, that you need to pay attention to the gift you have in each other, then take this as one now. Trust me, you don't want to look back and think about the one that got away."

My skin goes cool and a chill runs across my body. I'm beginning to feel like there's a design to this trip. Nice one, Aunt Hattie.

Well played.

ELEVEN

Amelia

They say good news travels fast, but bad news? Not only does it travel faster, but it also takes on a life of its own. This fact is currently being proven true while I sit here with my phone pressed to my ear, listening to Riley as her words tumble over each other.

"Slow down, Riley. Take a breath." I wait until she's quiet before speaking. "Now, you've seen photos of us online doing what?"

"The photos are not good," Riley growls in my ear. "You're standing with Barney at your feet, looking shocked, and Spencer's face is red, and he looks like he's confused with a dash of irritation. But the way the picture is taken it looks like he's yelling at you or just got done. I think the caption said something like 'Stoll Relationship Patrol: single or still together?' If it's not true, it makes me so mad, but if it is true, and he was yelling at you—"

"Well, he wasn't," I interrupt, smacking my hand to my forehead. "It was a two-way argument happening after we locked the keys in the RV. Since Barney is in the picture, the photo would have been taken after we got the keys back, so they actually missed the real argument."

She giggles. "Not trying to laugh at your situation, but it's crazy that you're on the road with the 'Sexiest Man Alive.'"

"Well, we'll see how sexy he feels when I tell him about this." Stretching my neck to one side, I look at the tiny space and ponder doing a few down dogs and giving my body some attention before Spencer gets back from walking Barney. My thoughts are interrupted when the door swings open and Barney comes bounding inside, Spencer poking his head in a moment later. Making eye contact with me, he holds his finger up, telling me he'll be back in a minute before disappearing again.

Riley and I talk for a few minutes more, with me thanking her for alerting us to the story, before I hang up and wait for Spencer to come back. He's not going to be thrilled with the news, and neither will his team. A team that includes his father who, I know from experience, will have the strongest and loudest opinions of all.

Pivoting in my seat, I get up and make my way to the bedroom to put on my pajamas. I made sure to get a shower and brush my teeth before Riley called, knowing I'd be crashing soon tonight.

I'm about to walk back to the table when I spy the package we'd gotten from Big Andy. Grabbing the cardboard box from the shelf above my bed, I sit down, spinning it in my hands. I can't tell from its size or weight what's inside. Shaking it, I put my ear close but hear nothing. Nada. Zip. I've got nothing for guesses about what it is.

Placing it on the mattress beside me, I hold myself back from opening it for a good two minutes before I give in to temptation. I'm at the kitchen drawer grabbing a knife and back attacking the box in no time. Pulling back the cardboard flaps, I pull out layer after layer of tissue paper and bubble wrap. Whatever Aunt Hattie put in here must be precious cargo, that's for sure.

Finally getting to the bottom, I stop when my hand hits something hard and smooth. Peeking in, I'm surprised to find an old photo album. Cocking my head to one side, I pull it out and turn it over in my hands. I've not seen it before.

Carefully, I open the cover to find another surprise: a handwritten inscription.

To Amelia and Spencer, may you always have your happily ever after for infinity. All my love, H.

Before I can turn the first page, the door to the RV swings open again, bringing in a blast of cold air and Spencer right along with it.

"Hey." Do I notice the grin that breaks over a worried expression suddenly? You bet I do. I notice it like I notice him sliding his phone in his back pocket. My gut does a little knock; I know his tells when he's trying to keep a secret. I have a sneaking suspicion he's been told about the photos showing up on social media already and is probably trying to figure out the best way to tell me.

"Hi," I call out. "You look like you just found out that there's photos of us going around."

Spencer sighs, running his fingers through his hair as he shakes his head. "I'm sorry, Amelia, you know it's part of this whole acting thing that I hate..."

"Stop. I mean it." Patting the empty space beside me, I motion for him to come to the back and join me. "Riley called and told me already."

"Dad was the one who called me." He rolls his eyes. "So, you can guess how well that went down."

"And he knows it'll blow over in a day or two, right?" I shrug. I'm not being flippant, I just know how the game works, and if Spencer pauses for a moment and thinks about it, so does he. "You've got those interviews coming up and you can address it then. Or you can go on your own social media and we can write up a post...but giving it more gas keeps the fire going. Right?"

"You're right." He's sheepish but he smiles my way. "I should just sit down and be here, now."

"Exactly. Be present." Patting the space on the bed again, I can sense his hesitation as Spencer eyes the seat next to me. "Seriously. Come and sit. Try to not think about it right now —in fact"—I hold the photo album up in the air—"you can look at this with me."

Spencer's eyes widen, and he points to the box. "Is that the first package?"

"Sure is. Wanna see?"

Pulling back the cover, I flip a few pages and my heart skips when I find the first photograph. It's one taken of me and Spencer on the day we were married on a suspended bridge. He's twirling me around in a circle and I'm holding on to him for dear life.

"I almost flipped us off the bridge that day," he murmurs, leaning closer to me and putting his chin on my shoulder.

"I remember." Turning the page, we're greeted by a picture of Aunt Hattie standing in between us, her golden hair threaded with silver streaks pulled back into a French braid, the three of us laughing together with the Hollywood sign behind us. "This was when she came out in the *Dream Chaser* to visit for a few days."

"She stayed on the West Coast for almost six months!" Spencer exclaimed. "That was when I first became interested in the RV life; she made it look cool. She came to see us in LA, then went off to San Fran, then went to—"

"Portland." I smile, my heart filling with memory after

memory like waves crashing to the shore. "I still have the coffee mug she got me at Powell's Bookstore. I flew up for a weekend and stayed in Portland with her and we spent one whole day at the bookstore, trawling it for books."

"Don't forget the time she went to work at the ski resort," Spencer says with a laugh, pointing to a photo when I flip another page. This picture was one I had taken of her and Spencer after an afternoon on the slopes. "Man, she had a life. You know? She lived."

"She did, and I love that when she passed, her orders were for us to celebrate her at all times and not on one day. That's why she didn't want a memorial, she didn't want us crying for her. She wanted us to live, laugh, love." Sighing, I turn another page, my hand hovering in the air as I let it go, staring at the couple in the photograph.

This couple is staring at one another as they stand on a porch at sunset. Her arms are intertwined around his neck and he has his wrapped around her, holding her close. You couldn't slip a piece of paper in between this couple, the love between them oozes off the page.

"Oh, wow." Spencer's words are like a whoosh as he breathes them out. "Look at that."

"I know." Using my forefinger, I trace the outline. Spencer's jaw is still as chiseled and perfect now as it was then. "We were so in love, Spencer."

Closing the album, I find Spencer staring at the floor as if he's lost in thought, watching his feet as they tap silently.

I can feel it inside me that it's time. One of us needs to take the proverbial bull by the horns here.

Tapping the album, I can't help but smile. "We were happy in these photos."

"Seeing you walking down the aisle to meet me on our wedding day..." Spencer pauses, looking for his words. "It's a moment I never want to have wiped from my memory. I can still feel the vise-like grip you had on my heart when I look at those photos."

My heart goes clunk. "Had?"

Standing, he takes his sweatshirt off and tosses it on the other single mattress. "I say 'had' because part of me thinks at the time I was infatuated with you. With us. With what could be."

Okay, this conversation is not going the way I thought it would. In fact, I think I'm feeling a little bit uncomfortable right now. Spencer takes a few steps into the kitchen area, where he hits the button to bring his bed down. Once the tiny motor stops and the bed is in place, he turns around to face me and leans his back against it.

"I don't like that you say 'had,' Spencer. And I know it's counterintuitive to how I've acted—"

"Ah. Are we talking about the divorce papers now?" Tugging off his shirt, he pulls it over his head, leaving me with Spencer Stoll and his super sexy six-pack.

How on earth am I going to be able to have any kind of conversation with this man now, when he's standing in front of me looking like he's been working out for the last year nonstop? I know he did this on purpose. My eyes drag across his chest, taking in its full glistening glory. The firm sculpture of his muscles makes me wonder if I can crack a pecan on them. There's a primal urge to reach out and drag my fingers across his chest, but I resist.

"I am talking about those papers, yes." I manage to swallow, a feat I didn't think I could muster considering how dry my mouth is all of a sudden. "I...*we* have so much we need to talk about."

"*We* do, but for now maybe we should try to get some rest." Turning his back to me, I feel his pain rippling through the small space. The papers I sent out of anger, after promising for both of us that we'd not jump to anything that drastic unless we had to. It's at this moment, I'm seeing that my fifty percent of this equation needs to involve some serious apologizing if we're going to get anywhere.

Spencer goes to throw his leg up on the bed to hoist himself up and into it, only a cracking sound fills the air as his knee(?) connects with part of the frame. Like a pinball, he bounces backward on one leg, hopping on the good one and trying to hold the one he's hurt. Barney watches him by his feet, wincing and trying to stay out of his way in the small space.

"Be careful of Barney," I offer. Is that the best I can do?

"Yeah, thanks," he growls, glowering my way. "I'm fine, don't worry about me."

"Oh, come on, Spencer. You know I didn't mean it like that." I start to stand up, but the space is more compact now with the bed in its place for the night. Slamming myself back on the bed, I flick my hand in his direction. "Put that bed back up in the ceiling and just sleep on the other twin bed in here."

His back to me, Spencer wince-hops a few more times before he turns around and looks at me again. He inclines his head in the direction of the bed. "You sure you're okay with me sleeping there tonight?"

I nod. "It's two twin beds next to each other. That's all."

He eyes me suspiciously for a moment until he finally grabs the blanket off his bed and presses the button, securing the spare back into its hiding spot above the dining table. The RV is really well laid out, I can give it that.

While he gets settled on the bed, I get Barney into his spot by my feet. Once I know everyone is where they need to be, and even though I really want to keep the conversation going right now, I turn off the light. Some things you don't want to push.

Lying in bed, I toss and turn a few times, finally settling on my back so I can stare into the darkness above me.

"'Melia?" Spencer whispers.

"Yes?"

"You know, it's not a bad thing that you 'had' such a hold on me when we got married." There's a rustling sound as he sits up in his bed, throwing his legs over the side. "I say had because it was infatuation, and to me that's so much different than being in love. You know?"

"Yeah." I roll on my side and use my hand to prop up my head so I can see his silhouette in the dark. "I think I do."

"I need to explain this, I want to." He leans closer to me, his elbows on his knees. The tiny space is so close I can feel his breath on my cheek. "I want you to understand I crossed into this wide expanse of emotion the day I met you. I always knew I wanted to find love, but after a while, going on dates and trying to meet people, I'd written it off. I figured things would be easier if it was just me, right? My dad was always saying that anyway. No one else to take care of, I could just be totally selfish and only take care of myself."

Chuckling, I push myself up so I can throw my legs over the side of my bed, too. "That I can understand. I think I was also in a similar place when we met."

I wriggle around to find a comfortable position but manage to knock my knees into his. Before I can move them again, hands reach out taking either side of my thighs, and he stills me as he slides a leg in between mine so we're sand-wiched. A fluttering effect rages through me and across my skin, leaving an electric charge at the roots of my hair.

"Stay here." His voice husky, I feel his fingers dig into the outside of my thighs, but I can't be mad at it. We sit like this, threaded together and so close I can smell the clean crispness of his soap, for what feels like hours but in reality, of course, only minutes pass.

My hands rest on my knees as his massage their way up my legs, onto my lap where he takes both of my hands in his and pulls me to him, so we meet in the middle. The warmth of his hand is like a searing poker to my skin as he lets his fingers dance their way up my arm, stroking the insides by my elbow and the vulnerable smooth skin of my inner arm.

The groan that escapes my lips is one I can't take back. Closing my eyes, I lean forward, wanting to press myself closer, wanting his arms to wrap around me solidly, to hold me close.

Spencer's fingers are in my hair, twining pieces as he presses his forehead to mine. The heat of his breath hits my lips as I slide my nose across his. Willingly, gratefully, and wholeheartedly, I go limp in his arms as he tugs me closer and slants his lips across mine.

As my lips part and Spencer's softness presses down on mine, I drag my hands up to either side of his face, holding him still and cradling his cheeks in my hands. My thumbs softly caress his jawline as my breath hitches inside me, coming out in short bursts as I fight against all of the instincts roaring to life within me.

Gasping for air, I pull back and hold him at arm's length. We sit quietly, his chest rising and falling as rapidly as mine.

"You okay?" He squeezes my hand, and even in the dark, I know the thoughtful expression that's on his face. "Tell me if I need to slow down, Amelia. Tell me what you're thinking."

"I'm thinking we need to slow down." I squeeze his hand back and pull further away, pushing my fingers through my hair. So much electricity is sparking inside of me right now, I don't know how to contain it or if I even want to. "And I think we need some sleep. Right now. That's what I think."

He's quiet, his head dips. I know, I'm the fun police right now, but if we're going to accomplish anything between us, there are some elephants in the room we need to address first.

It all seemed so clear a few months back. It's true what they say, that out of sight is out of mind, and I'm beginning to realize I pushed him to go to LA so I could get him out of my mind. There's an internal struggle happening between my head and my heart, which is still bruised...or maybe that's my ego?

"Okay, then." There's movement across from me as he retreats, the rustling of the sheets tells me he's back under them. "I'm going to hit pause...for now."

Fluffing my pillow, I arrange myself back under my comforter as well and lay my head down. "Thank you."

"I said, for now," he growls, that sexy huskiness back in his tone. "I'm not here to give up, Amelia. I'm here to see things through, but for right now—we pause. Because when you're ready..."

"If." I throw a hand in the air, not sure if he can even see it, but it's there.

"Fine, when and if, but we both know it's more of a when. I need you to know I'm going to trail kisses up and down your neck, stopping only to let the heat of my breath fall across your earlobe as I pull you close to me and slowly, ever so slowly and, in a way where you can't escape me, I'll begin to unbutton your..."

What is he trying to do to me now? "And with that, I bid you goodnight," I say emphatically before rolling over and putting my back to him.

Over the past year, I convinced myself I wasn't supposed to be with this man. I've told myself he's selfish, we don't want the same things, and that the connection was lost. I thought space and distance would help me close the part of my heart he'd cracked open so many years ago.

But man was I wrong. Like, so wrong. Because here I am. Lying almost beside him and wanting him back in my arms, wanting for me to be held in his. Here I am thinking we can make it work because we have what it takes to go the long haul.

But, yet, here I am. Asking for a divorce from a man I'm clearly, most definitely, quite certainly, and unequivocally still in love with.

TWELVE

Spencer

"Pass me the Twizzlers?" Thrusting my hand in Amelia's direction for the third time in the last ten minutes, I think it's fair to say I'm eating my emotions. I've been doing a good job of it since we left Stone Mountain earlier.

Let's discuss why I'm feeding my feelings: I've got a phone interview tomorrow for my latest film releasing over the holidays, I'm in an RV with the woman of my dreams, who runs simultaneously hot and cold, and I'm fighting off leg cramps from having been in a sitting position for hours on end over the last few days.

Yep. Seems about right.

"Here you go." Amelia plunks the package in the palm of my hand before she goes back to fighting with a map, folding it and re-folding it over and over until she gets it to the right size so she can read it.

"I know you're enjoying studying that thing, but why don't you pull up the GPS on your phone?"

"Because, Captain Obvious, if I was busy looking at my

phone, I never would have found..." She pauses dramatically before doing a drumroll on her legs. "Sunflower Falls!"

From the tone and excitement conveyed, I feel like I'm supposed to know what Sunflower Falls is.

"Yay?" I manage, sadly, pumping a solo fist in the air.

"Not just 'yay,' Spencer. I've seen pictures of this place, and it's stunning. Sunflower Falls was used as the backdrop for *The Hunger Games* and *Last of the Mohicans.*" She leans over and gives my arm a light punch. "I figured you of all people would dig this. You loved *The Hunger Games.*"

She's right. I read the books, saw the movies, and whenever they're on television, I stop everything to watch them. Is it odd that I find them soothing?

Also, that statement, right when she said "you of all people would dig this?" That tells me she's thinking about me. Let's hold on to that feeling for a second, Spencer, and not let it go.

"All right, then. I'm listening and color me intrigued." I throw a wink in her direction. "How much farther?"

Her mouth crinkles as it unfolds into the brightest smile I've seen from this woman in a long time. "If we take the next exit, it's about ten miles off the main road."

"And you're sure we have time to stop?"

Looking at the clock, I start to second-guess things. It's getting late, not so late that it's night soon, but we're approaching dusk. Last thing I want is for us to be still on the road when it gets dark. We both need to get used to driving the RV first, so in my mind, daytime trips are the smartest.

Well, look at me thinking about things. Assuming she's keeping me around. There's hope in my heart, especially after last night. I know she feels what I do—you can't turn off feelings like we had for each other like a garden hose or a television. I know this, says the man who's eaten his weight in Twizzlers just today alone.

All this tells me I'm going to give her no choice but to keep me around.

"We have time to stop," she murmurs, tapping the map. "It's kind of isolated where it's located, so I'm thinking there won't be a lot of other visitors out there this time of year. We drive in, find the falls, hang out for a breather, and then we're back on the road. One and done in about thirty minutes."

"Well, then." I flick on the blinker, her point now made, changing lanes and grinning. "Let's go see Sunflower Falls."

Amelia's directions are impeccable; we're there in about ten minutes. The drive into the park takes another five minutes or so, winding our way to the back where the falls are, the path on one side leading into a dense forest, and on the other, we see glimpses of water through the breaks in the trees.

I can't park fast enough. We're out of the RV, smelling of earth and nature around us, walking in silent reverence with only the noise of the waterfall in the distance to greet us, its music calling us closer. Amelia points to a trail off the small parking lot and heads toward it, Barney at her side, and me taking up the rear.

The path isn't very long, and within a few moments' time, the forest around us opens up, revealing the majestic Sunflower Falls. And it's beautiful: water cascading over a rocky cliff, spilling and creating a shimmering fall of a liquid crystal blue. The late afternoon sun rays hit drops of mist dancing in the air, making prismatic rainbows dance in front of us.

Amelia stands with one hand on her hip and holding Barney's leash in the other, her hair pulled back and sunglasses pushed on top of her head. The smile draping across those lips of hers makes my heart skip a beat. "So, are you glad we stopped?"

I'd be happier if I could hold you in my arms right now, kiss your neck, and...

Instead, I nod. "So happy."

"We're not doing too bad on time, either." Amelia checks her watch. "Let's head back to the motorhome and get out of here."

We trod down the path together, this time Amelia slows down to keep pace beside me, our hands bouncing into each other as we walk side by side. The first few times it happens, I figure she doesn't mean to do it. When it happens a fifth time, I grab her hand and close it tightly in mine, half-expecting her to snatch it back. But she doesn't.

We walk like this, hand in hand, all the way back to the RV, which I consider a win since she doesn't pull away until we're right on top of it. There's a buoyant feeling deep in my tummy doing a happy dance as I walk around to the driver's side and take one last look around before I hop behind the wheel. Around us, the late afternoon sun is starting to set, the trees casting dappled shadows across the forest floor. It'll be dark soon, so it's great we're leaving now.

Turning the ignition over, I wait for the familiar sound; the rattle and hum of the engine coming to life. It's usually a gradual awakening, with its diesel engine taking a second or two to turn over.

Only, it doesn't. It's not coming to life.

Twisting the key once more, I try again. This time, I look at Amelia with my face pinched and her eyes wide as I turn it over.

Nothing.

"No way." She shakes her head as Barney curls up in his makeshift bed on the floor between our seats. "Could the engine be flooded?"

I look down at my feet. "I'm not pumping the gas."

"I swear, this trip is cursed." She digs her phone out of her bag. "I'll call triple A and see if we can get towed—nope. Won't be doing that."

"What?" I crane my neck in her direction. "Why?"

She holds her phone in the air and lets it drop to the floor at her feet. "No service."

Laughter involuntarily bubbles to the surface. "You're joking."

"Wish I was." She places her forehead on the window and sighs. "It's getting darker out there. I'm going to jog up the road a little ways to see if I can get any service, or maybe someone else is here and we can ask them for help."

Peering out the window at the trees surrounding us, one thought comes into my mind. "Don't most horror movies have someone in the group who is like 'I'm gonna go get help' and then they are found flayed in the bushes later?"

"You're such a positive ray of light." Amelia shakes her head as she opens the door and jumps out. "Why don't you bring Barney, then, and come with me?"

Not a bad idea. "Sounds good."

In a few moments, we've backtracked on the dirt road toward the park entrance, Amelia beside me holding her phone up and saying, "No. No...no, no, no," every few seconds as she waits for the heavens to send us a bar of service. Closing her eyes, she opens her mouth, silently screaming, as she stops by a signpost with a map of the park attached and leans against it.

"This is futile." She looks at the map on the post and points to the park entrance. "Looks like the main gates where we came in are right around the bend there." She points just beyond the trees where we're currently standing. "Maybe someone's there."

Racking my brain, I can't recall seeing a park ranger station nor another person since we got off the road and entered the Sunflower Falls park. She jogs ahead to the bend to look, my stomach sinking when she stops, hangs her head, and jogs back to us looking defeated.

"The gate to the park is shut." She looks at me with trepidation. "We're locked in here, Spencer."

The low tremble in her voice tells me she's rattled. "Okay, well let's get back to the RV and..."

"And what?" she snaps. "We can't do anything."

"We have a house on wheels, Amelia. We're going to sleep in it and deal with this in the morning." I look at the sky above. "It's getting dark, our hands are tied."

"Someone has to come along..."

"Not necessarily. If those park gates are closed, someone has come along already and locked them. Then they probably went home to their family." Taking the lead, I start walking back in the direction of the RV. "Come on. We've got enough charge to use electricity, and we have potable water."

Amelia stops in her tracks behind me. "Will we be okay?"

"It's what that motorhome was made for. Boondocking. It's also called freedom camping in other parts of the world." I walk a few steps back to where she stands and wrap my arms around her. "I've got you, okay? Nothing is going to happen to you."

When she shoots me a sideways glance, I choose to ignore it.

Because we're calm. We've got this.

Right?

"But I don't want to use the toilet in here." Amelia stands outside the tiny bathroom, arms crossed and looking like a petulant child. Someone's hit a wall and isn't handling the small space any longer.

Give you two guesses who it is and, nope, it ain't Barney.

Inclining my head toward the door, I shrug a shoulder. "If you don't want to use the toilet in here, you're more than welcome to go outside into the cold night air and let loose next to any and all critters who happen to be in the woods tonight."

Amelia glares at me before she hops up and perches on the bed. "You could make it sound less menacing, and more Snow White."

"This is a mini-home, Amelia. It comes equipped for a reason. You're supposed to use the facilities."

"Not if we're staying in a campground," she huffs.

"Well, then, what am I thinking?" Smacking my head, I put a hand on my hip and stare at Barney. "We'd better fire this thing up and get on the road, so Princess can use the commode."

The muffled snort coming from Amelia's general direction is a good sign. She may be frustrated, but there's humor.

"I'm not a princess."

"You packed three suitcases." Opening the refrigerator, I pull out an apple and take a bite. "And don't tell me you didn't pack heels because I saw them. Did you think we were going to a ball?"

"Fine, I overpacked. And no, I don't want to use the toilet in here because it's literally two feet from the kitchen sink!"

Standing still, I rotate in a circle. "Everything in this thing is two feet from the kitchen sink."

Grunting with frustration, Amelia jumps to her feet. "Fine. I'm going to use it, but I need you to go to the front of the RV. To the driver's seat and turn on some music, please."

Nodding, I take a few steps and throw myself in the driver's seat, looking out the window. "I'll be right here, giving you privacy, until you're done, okay?"

The slamming of the door is all the answer I need. She's always been like this, very particular. When we first met years ago, I'd tried to get Amelia to venture out camping with me, but she always said no. To her, camping is a hotel without room service.

A loud smack pulls my attention to the back of the mobile home. "You okay?"

Another smack, a thud, and the bathroom door swings open and Amelia eases herself out.

"Look at that," I say, turning around in my seat, clapping my hands together. "You did it."

"I don't want to talk about it," she says, glaring at me as she throws herself into the dining table booth and lays her head against the side of the RV, looking out the window.

"Fine. Me neither." Biting into the apple, I chew as quietly as I can but keep one eye on her. She must have felt me, because she shudders, turns in her seat, and glowers in my direction.

"You make me crazy. This"—she waves her hands in the air around her—"is too much. I feel penned in. In a box."

"In a box, with a fox, eating lox?" Her face tells me my attempt at humor doesn't sit well.

"There it is, you finding the funny and me feeling uptight, like I should relax more and I'm wrong for being anxious." She shakes her head. "We used to be so good, you and I. One ended where the other one began, like yin and yang, and somewhere along the way everything got complicated and heavy."

Her words make me sit up a lot straighter. Did not know we were going to veer this way, but it's a direction we need to go if we're going to get through the mud.

"I fully take my part in this, Amelia. I know I closed up and backed away." Getting up out of my seat, I make my way over to her, sliding into the seat beside her. "Backed away sounds nicer than ran away, doesn't it?"

She turns to face me, her eyes flashing with anger. "You ran at light speed, Spencer. I said baby, you said 'buh-bye' and it rattled me. I said I wanted support so I could start a new business, and you took off for the other side of the country."

"It's work, Amelia. I had to go, you know how fickle the entertainment industry is. You're hot until you disappear, and I need to be around for meetings, to work on the film, and to provide some stability for us while I can, because you know as well as I do nothing lasts forever."

"You're right," she whisper-spits with a hint of venom. "Nothing lasts forever."

Seeing the look on her face, I know where she's going with this. "No, no, get out of your head. If you think I was saying something subliminal to you, you're wrong." Grabbing her, I put a hand on each shoulder. "Look at me, Amelia, look into my eyes and look. At. Me."

She drags her eyes to meet mine, green flecks dancing across honey-brown eyes and framed by the longest eyelashes ever. There's a cluster of freckles across the bridge of her nose that I've always loved, and right now, I want to lean in and place a kiss on each and every one of them.

"This is not how we used to be." Leaning in, I kiss her forehead, feeling her stiffen as I do. "What happened?"

She takes a breath, letting it out slowly. "You left."

"And I'll spend every day for the rest of our lives working to make that up to you." I kiss her right cheek, leaning my forehead against hers and touching nose to nose. "I'm back if you'll have me."

Kissing her other cheek, I rest my forehead on hers again as she sighs. "What if we're too late?"

"Don't say that." My heart seizes as I pull back, looking hard into her eyes. "We are and we can be how we used to be. We're still who we are at our core, we just need to readjust our goalposts a little, and I need to apologize a lot, but we are still who we used to be."

Cocking her head to one side, she leans and tips my chin with her forefinger. "Then, show me."

"Show you what?"

Grabbing my top, she clutches the fabric and pulls me into her. "Show me how we used to be."

"I thought you'd never ask." My hands fly up to her head, not even slowing down for fear she'll rebuke me. I wrap my fingers through her hair, pulling her mouth onto mine, and I swear I can taste the sweetness of sugar cookies and caramel syrup all mixed together as I let myself get lost.

Amelia's primal groan as she arches her back and crashes her body into mine threatens to shatter my resolve, not that I should have any, right? But of course I do, I want to have some. As much as I want her, I've been gone and there's work to do, I'm not just going to expect her to let me back in because I can kiss real good...but I'm going to do my best to make it count for at least ninety percent of this equation.

There's a fantasy I've had in my mind this past year where I come back to Amelia, pull her into my arms, and beg for forgiveness so we can start over. I'm realizing now starting over means being who we were then, and I want her as she is now.

Her hands trail along my arms, her fingernails lightly clawing across my skin, stoking fire to my wild drive, but I resist. Slowing down, our kisses take a more languid pace, and pressing my lips firmly to her forehead, I pull away.

And that my friends, is how you shut your wife up. With love and kisses.

I push a stray hair away from her cheek. "I'm sorry, I don't want to push you or add any pressure."

She holds her hand up to stop me, then pushes me gently. "Can you let me out?"

Worried I'm moving too fast, which is weird to think about when you're married, but not really when you need to tread carefully, as I do. It's a dance for us here, and I'm treating this like I'm wooing her all over again.

I watch as she walks to the back of the RV. I'm thrilled when she turns around, motioning for me to follow her.

Climbing into bed, she watches me as I flick off the lights, eyeing me more as I climb onto the single bed opposite her. I point to the space between us where the piece of mattress fits to make this a king bed. "Don't think of crossing that cavern there now, just 'cause I kissed you and I kissed you good."

She sits up, flicking the lights back on, and hops off the bed, disappearing into the front of the RV. I hear the storage compartment open that's next to the fridge, more rustling. When she appears again, she holds the small section of mattress in her hands and grins.

Placing it on its tracks, she locks it in, then climbs back into her side of the bed, both of us still fully dressed. Flipping the covers back, she curls up and lies on her side, her back facing me. I scooch forward, tentatively wrapping my arms around her middle, but Amelia takes them and pulls them around her, pulling me closer so I can cradle her against me.

The last thing I remember is the tiny sigh escaping from her lips as we both give in to sleep, and go to where only our dreams can take us.

Together.

THIRTEEN

Spencer

Morning came a lot faster than I wanted it to. We'd woken up, tangled in each other's arms and smiling. I wasn't sure if it was only me, but I swear the energy in the motorhome seemed to have shifted like a storm had moved past us and was on to its next destination, leaving a bright globe of sunshine overhead.

By the time we'd made coffee and had breakfast, luckily someone else traveling for the holidays stopped to see the falls. One jump-start later, and we were back on the road. Our morning routine couldn't have gone smoother. Glancing at the digital clock on the dash, I let out an internal whoop of gratitude. We'll be at our next stop in plenty of time for my interview, so that'll make my LA team very happy and keep my father from blowing a gasket.

"Hey," Amelia begins, taking me away from my thoughts, "I hate to even suggest it, but we need to pull over before we get to Ramblin' Ricks."

Wiggling my eyebrows, I throw a wink her way. "Are you in need of more time in nature?"

"Oh no." Chuckling, she points to my key ring. "We need to get a spare key."

She's right. Glancing at the fuel levels, we have over a half tank left, so we won't need to refuel, which is helpful. Less stops, the better. I'm about to pull my eyes away when a red light begins flashing, lighting up a symbol I've not seen before.

I lean forward and tap on the dashboard. "Can you pull out the manual and see what this light means?"

Amelia opens the glovebox, grabs the operating manual, and starts flipping through its pages. She's quiet as she finds what she's looking for. She turns in her seat to get a better look at the symbol, looks back at the book, then back at the symbol again, grunting her displeasure.

"It's for the toilet." She taps the book. "It says here when that light comes on, we need to empty the toilet cassette."

Well, we knew this day would come. "Really?"

She nods. "Didn't Gerry say we should stop as soon as it comes on or at least deal with it sooner rather than later?" Amelia grabs her phone and starts tapping away. She lifts her head triumphantly a moment later.

"Looks like there's a dumping station—their term, not mine—where we can empty that thing, and right across the road we can also get a spare key made, all at the same time." She points to a sign as we speed past it on the highway. "There. Exit 64 in ten miles."

I fight the urge to floor it, not so much for the toilet cassette but more for the fact I just want to get where we're going. If you've ever seen the old TV show *Gilligan's Island*, I'm feeling like that crew. What started out as a "three-hour tour" is turning into Gulliver's Travels. I'm beginning to think we've entered some kind of alternate universe where we're stuck driving in this thing for all eternity. Not that it would be so bad, I'm okay with the company, but I'm sure the Groundhog Day of it all would get to one of us eventually.

It's not long until we're off the highway and find the road-side stop we've been looking for. There's a small hardware store that has disposal facilities for RVs and campervans to drop their waste, but you can also do some shopping if you need supplies. Someone was very smart when planning this business.

"So," Amelia begins, opening the passenger side door and letting Barney out first. "Not it!"

"Did you really just declare a 'not it' moment?"

Her eyes dancing with glee, she blows me a kiss. "I'll get the key made, you can empty the"—she waves her hand in the air and makes a face—"thing."

"Isn't marriage all about sharing our experiences, the good and the bad?"

"Please. This is one experience you can tell me about later." She slams the door closed, laughing. Opening my door, I hop out as well, shutting the door behind me. She walks around and holds her hand out to me expectantly.

"Keys?"

With a sick feeling rolling across my stomach, I try the door handle. It's locked. I walk around to the door that enters into the kitchen area. Locked, too. I don't have to check Amelia's door to know it's gonna be locked as well. It's a blessing and a curse that this thing has an automatic locking mechanism.

Note to self: TURN IT OFF.

I close my eyes and slowly bang my head against the side of the RV while Amelia bites her lip.

"Again?"

I can tick "boosting wife yet again to roof" off my road-trip bingo card. One quick trip for her inside the hardware store and we've got our spare key. Finally. Amelia even went so far as to get a hide-a-key with a super-charged magnet on it so we can put the spare under one of our tire wells. Future crises now averted, and yes, my fingers are crossed as I say that.

But now, the time has come for me to do what men like me have done in times gone by: I need to empty this toilet waste so we can get back on the road, and I need to do it *without* dry heaving.

Amelia directs as we drive across the road to where a line of RVs sit cued and waiting. "The guy in the hardware store told me that we need to get in line and wait our turn. When we get to the waste disposal, we'll pull the container out using the outside compartment, undo the lid of the cassette, and then you tip it out and empty it in the hole."

"Empty it in the hole." My eyes rock back to hers. "I guess the hole is what everyone is waiting in line for?"

She nods, chewing that gorgeous full pink lip of hers. "When it's empty, put the lid back on, and then slide it back into the compartment."

She makes it sound so easy, but there's a look on her face like she's smelled something bad. Looking at me with eyes wide and full of faux innocence, she puts two fingers on her lips, making a look like a blowfish as if she's holding back her breakfast, and then makes quiet retching sounds.

"Thanks." I look in front of us, satisfied that the line is moving pretty quickly. "Lots of people here for this time of year."

"That's what I thought, too, but the guy inside said it's like this all the time around the holidays. Summer is busier, of course, but not by much."

My cell phone dings from its spot on the center console.

"Do you mind seeing who it is?" I ask Amelia.

She swipes it, scanning the screen. "It's a text from Bex, reminding you of your interview in a few hours."

Sighing, I scrunch my lips. "Oh. Yeah. That."

"You don't sound thrilled."

"I don't mind talking to reporters about the projects, and I know it's part of my job, but this time, it's different." I turn slightly in my seat so I can face Amelia. "I don't want to waste time talking to them. Not when I can spend that time talking to you."

There's a range of emotions washing across her features. I want to say so much more, but the honking of a horn behind me tells me I need to pay attention to my surroundings.

Amelia glares in her side mirror. "Great. We've got some pushy camping enthusiasts behind us."

Pulling up next to the receptacle, I make sure I'm parked in the right spot before turning off the engine. "We'll be out of here soon. Give me a few minutes to deal with this. Wish me luck."

Closing the door behind me, I make sure I've got my keys. Check. I'm going to need them to unlock the compartment door on the outside of the RV so I can get the toilet cassette out, which I've now done. Check.

I walk around the RV to the receptacle and find a scene straight out of a high school reunion film: there's a few other RVs and camper vans parked nearby with small groups of people milling about. Some stand in line to use the same facilities I'm about to, and others are just talking to friends or fellow motorhoming people. Sharing road stories, I'm sure.

Pulling my baseball hat out of my back pocket, I pull it on tight over my head, praying no one recognizes me here. Not when I'm dealing with number ones and twos, amIright?

Like the line to gain access, the line for emptying the cassette moves quickly. Quicker than I thought because I don't have much time to watch other people and see how they do it. So when it comes my turn, I think back to what Amelia said we do and chuckle to myself.

Still holding the keys in one hand, I stand by the hole in the ground and open the lid to the toilet cassette. Easy as pie. Turning the cassette over, I do the next step, tipping it over and emptying it. Boo-yah! It's going well. On the plus side, everyone around me is so busy having social time, no one pays any attention to me. We'll be out of here in a few seconds; no risk of any photos to fuel a gossip mill and no stopping for autographs. Luck is on my side today.

Once I'm satisfied the cassette is empty, I look around for the lid to replace it, finding it on the ground, dangerously close to the giant hole...otherwise known from here on out as the "place where the sun don't shine" and also the place where we do not want to drop the lids.

I reach across and swipe at the lid, only as I do this, one of the keys on the ring I'm still gripping in my hands for life support suddenly breaks skin and pierces the palm of my hand. The pain is intense and immediate, causing me to cry out in pain as I open my hand, dropping them.

It's like a slow-motion scene straight from a film: our keys, which were in my hand a mere moment before, tumble and fall to the ground and bounce...right into the waste receptacle, disappearing from view.

Staring at the hole in the ground, a feeling of water flushes (pun intended) through my veins. It's icy cold and adds to the shock I'm feeling.

There's a trio of older men leaning against an old Airstream trailer, and one of them has me in his sights. "Huh. That's going to cause an issue."

"You think?" Okay, that came out a bit terse, but, dude—I just lost my keys to a literal black hole.

"You know, it's not a straight pipe there," one of the other men says, his Southern twang coming through. "It curves about a foot down, so if you can get something in there, you may be able to get your keys out."

Squinting, I look at the three men, then back in the hole. "Really?"

"Yep." A female voice joins the chorus. When I peer up, a couple of older women, grandmotherly types, are peeking out of the doorway of the Airstream.

"You're gonna need to be MacGyver to get them out, though," another one chimes in with a cackle.

Someone taps my shoulder. "Spencer?"

Turning around, I'm beyond relieved to see Amelia. She looks at me, at the hole in the ground, then at the small crowd around me. There are whispers from the women, and I hear my name. Worried someone's recognized me, I exchange a look with Amelia.

She steps closer, plastering a tight smile on her face and speaking through gritted teeth. "What's going on?"

"Looks like he dropped your keys down on everyone's waste." Not having heard this voice before, I crank my neck to the right and find a young girl, probably around the age of sixteen, smirking our way while she holds her phone in her hand. I can already see the social media posts.

"We can fix this." Amelia looks at the scene before her, then to me. "Give me a sec."

Spinning on her heel, she walks with purpose around to the other side of the motorhome. I hear the door slam and watch as the small unit shakes with her weight and movement as she walks around looking for something, I assume.

I scan my eyes at the small crowd around me, nodding my head and putting one hand on my hip. I'm about to recite Lincoln's address to break the silence when I hear Amelia call out in a sing-song voice as she comes back around the corner of the RV.

"Alright, it's time to go fishing!" She's got a soup ladle duck-taped to a broom handle, and a huge grin on her face. She marches up beside me and holds the contraption out like she's presenting me with an Academy Award, and I've never been happier. But that's not the only reason why.

Standing on her tiptoes, she plants a kiss on my cheek as she pulls the hat down even lower on my head, shielding me. It's a small thing that makes a big impact as my heart slams in my chest. She grins up at me.

"We've got this."

FOURTEEN

Amelia

I don't think I'll ever be as excited as I am now pulling into the parking lot of Ramblin' Rick's. It's a bustling happy place, with people dressed in their warmest winter layers and milling about everywhere. Outside of the reception area, one woman is arranging rows of Poinsettia and another is busy hanging wreaths on the door and windows, and across the small driveaway outside of what looks like a dining hall, men are on ladders hanging Christmas lights.

When I fling open the door and hop out, I'm giddy hearing the sounds of Christmas carols playing over loudspeakers. Sniffing the air, I swear I'm picking up on scents of cinnamon mixed with pine, and it's nothing short of amazing.

"Oh, wow." Spencer stands next to me, surveying the scene before us. "Where are we?"

Pointing to the building clearly marked "Women's bathroom and shower" I whisper, "Heaven?"

"Feels more like Santa's workshop." Spencer chuckles, putting an arm around my waist as he presses his lips close to my ear—dangerously close. "I'm pretty happy to finally be here, too."

Someone behind us clears their throat, giving me a jump-scare moment and even stopping my heart for a brief second. Spinning on my heel, there's a guy standing in front of us who looks a little too much like the Billy Bob Thornton version of St. Nick, his semi-dirty Santa hat sliding off his head as he picks his teeth with what looks to be a metal toothpick.

"Hey there," he says, tucking the toothpick into his pants pocket and pulling a clipboard out from under his arm. "Welcome, welcome. Let's get you signed in. What name is your reservation under?"

"Oh." Glancing back at Spencer, probably for a little strength, I step toward the resident Bad Santa. "I don't think we have one."

"Uh-oh. " His green eyes flicker with concern like I just asked one of his elves to add one more present to the sleigh before the Christmas run. "I'm sorry, but I don't think we have any space left. We get really full this time of year."

"Really?" Spencer croaks, his face conveying the same surprise currently shocking my system as well. Eyeing the RV, my stomach sinks. The last thing either of us needs is to be out attempting another night on our own and unsupervised in the wild.

The man nods, waving his hand at the organized chaos around us. "We do a special 'Christmas at the Campground' program. Christmas lights, caroling, hot chocolate. Santa Claus has a little house on the other side of the lot for photos, and"—he inclines his head toward a small open garden shed with a lean to the left—"there's an interactive nativity scene that folks come from miles around to see."

"Oh, wow." My heart sinks. One contingency we hadn't thought about on the road was what to do if we get here and it's full.

"And you're totally booked?" Spencer asks.

"Well, we don't have space for the RV, but we may have a

room left in our motel." He looks us both over, head to toe. "You'll be sharing a bathroom with other guests, though."

"It's fine." I turn to Spencer. "Once we get settled, I'll go find Rick and ask about getting the *Dream Chaser* looked at to make sure the battery won't cause us any issues again. There's got to be a mechanic—."

"Hold on," the man interjects as he pulls a half-eaten candy cane out of another pocket. "You didn't mention you were in the *Dream Chaser*."

Spencer and I exchange a look as I turn my hands around and shrug my shoulders. "I didn't know we had to?"

Santa chuckles. "If you're in the *Dream Chaser*, then you're here to find me, aren't you?"

"You're Rick?" Spencer asks.

"I am." He dips into a low curtsey the royal family would be proud of. "The one and only. I was a bona fide confidant of the woman who owned that RV for many years."

His sing-song voice is a touch of contrast to his whole outer vibe, and it makes me feel oddly comforted. "I'm Amelia, and my aunt has post-mortem sent us to you."

"Yes, she sure did, didn't she?" He laughs, taking the hat off his head. "I hoped you'd get here before the end of the year but certainly didn't expect you to come this close to Christmas."

"We've had extenuating circumstances," Spencer says. "In fact, do you know a mechanic who could look at our motorhome?"

In a flash, Rick is on his mobile phone calling one of his pals to swing by and look at the RV today, while simultaneously motioning for us to grab our things, and Barney, and follow him. We do as we're told, winding down a trail behind the reception office to a clearing in the woods where four motel-like units sit, tucked off to the side of the camping area.

"Okay," he says, disconnecting the call and pulling out his keys to hand us one. "Jim'll be here soon."

Moving in between us, he inserts the key in the lock, pushing the door open. I don't know if I've ever seen a bed that looks as comfy as this one does at this very moment. It's like I can hear angels sing as fireworks go off in the sky overhead. Not really, but it's still thrilling.

"I hate to chuck you in here and run, but as you can tell, it's chaotic. I need to go see if Mary's baby is up to par for our scene tomorrow night and I'm pretty sure one of the Wise Men could be in jail for not paying a jaywalking fine." He looks at Spencer and winks. "Actors, right?"

Spencer's cheeks flush bright red as Rick then treats us to a grin showing off a mouthful of sparkling white teeth, winking at me. "I've got something to give you from Hattie. I'll make sure you get it before you have to leave, but for now, get settled. We'll eat around five—we do it family style, all together in the dining hall."

With a wave of his hand, Rick is gone. As soon as he closes the door, Spencer launches himself onto the bed, kicking his feet in the air. "Solid mattress for a motel room." Sitting up, he turns around and smacks the pillows. "Oh, they feel good, too. Firm."

"Sleeping in a room without wheels is going to be a treat tonight, isn't it?" Giggling, I park myself on a chair at the small table for two in one corner of the room and watch as Barney leaps onto the bed to snuggle against Spencer.

"I don't mind sleeping in the RV, but I'm really excited about sleeping here." He looks around the room, his face twisting. "You know, it's just one bed. I can ask for a trundle bed if it makes you feel better."

Considering the fact that last night it was all I could do to get myself to sleep, you would think I'd be more eager for one. The feel of his touch on my skin is like a feeling of heat and ice coursing through my body, with lingering effects that can last up to hours. I'd forgotten how he can wrap me around his little finger.

I used to think that the Spencer Effect was magic, his to giveth as he wished and taketh away when needed, but not to me. Only with others. I'd watch from the sidelines as he would draw people—his fans, the clerk at the grocery store, our dry cleaner, anyone—into his orbit, leaving them starstruck and captivated. It's how he's managed to stay working, even coming back bigger and better than before after taking time off out of the limelight.

Looking at him standing in front of me now, the shadow of a smile still lingers on his lips, and my heart skips. His magnetic charisma, that is my kryptonite...oh, who am I kidding, so is that sexy smile and the way he can make me laugh even when I'm really mad. That takes talent, and the man has it in spades.

We could ask for a trundle bed, keeping the divide where it is, but part of me is worn out with myself. I shake my head. "I'm sure we'll be fine."

Clapping his hands together, Spencer hops off the bed and looks at Barney, picking up one of his paws to give him a high-five. "It's a slow burn, Barn, but she's coming around."

Laughing, I grab a pillow off the chair beside me and chuck it at him, with Spencer moving last minute so it smacks the wall. There's something through the window that catches his attention, so he walks over to peer out, tapping on the glass.

"I think a tow truck pulled up," he says, zipping his jacket back up and putting a hand on the doorknob. "I'll go see."

Tossing one last grin my way, he disappears out the door, leaving me alone with my thoughts and our suitcases. Since I don't feel like thinking anymore, I get busy pulling a few things out that we need like Barney's food and water bowls, charging cords for our phones and computers, and a fresh set of clothes.

Everything in me wants a shower, but I wait, deciding instead to wash my face, pull my hair up into a loose bun on top of my head, and throw on a little makeup. What I thought would take five minutes, turns into forty-five, and yet Spencer's still not back. As soon as I'm done, I clip the leash on Barney and we head out to find Spencer.

Outside is a large green area, with two park benches at one end and a small play set complete with a slide at the other. Straining against the leash, Barney's attention is pulled to a man in the middle of the yard, who is playing with a couple of kids, a boy and a girl. The man runs around, ducking behind trees and playing hide and seek on the other side of the swing set. I'm about to keep walking on my quest to find Spencer when I realize the man playing with these two adorable kids is him.

Folks, there is nothing sexier than a man who has no problem with making a fool of himself. No way. I may even fight you if you disagree. He's rolled up his shirt sleeves, put his baseball hat on backward, and, in between bouts of laughter, is running around teaching them how to do a Wookie call. It all goes sideways, though, when the little girl manages to trip her brother, causing him to run off the grass toward a woman standing off to the side, who must be his mom.

Spencer turns his head to the side to laugh, and oh man. He's even got mud splattered on his cheek.

That's my guy. Work hard, play hard.

"Hey," he calls out when he sees me, jogging my way breathlessly. "Did you see those two? They're ruthless."

"Excellent Chewbacca impersonation." Someone nearby claps their hands. The woman who comforted the little boy walks over to join us, the two small kids in tow. "These two have been riding in a car for hours and needed to just run around, shout out loud, and be kids, so thanks for helping them. It's not every day they get to play with..."

"Entertainment Magazine's Sexiest Man Alive?" I chortle, used to the gawking, as I lean over and instinctively wipe the mud from Spencer's cheek with my thumb.

The woman screws her face up, looking at me like I have nine heads and my hair is made of snakes. "No. I was going to say play with cool adults, but..." She steps back and sizes Spencer up. "Come to think of it, you do look like that guy. Steven Spool right? I think that's his name."

I have to bite my lips so the laughter doesn't escape, while she says thank you again and the siblings wave goodbye to Spencer. Standing with Barney's leash still loose in my hand, I watch her walk away with the two kids on either side of her and wait for Spencer's reaction. When they're out of sight, he turns to me and pumps a fist in the air.

"It must feel good to *not* be recognized, huh?"

"You have no idea." There's a faint beeping in his pocket that makes Spencer stop, pulling his phone out of his jacket. He reads the screen, his lips drawing into a tight line as he shoves the phone back.

"That doesn't look like it was good news."

Spencer shakes his head. "It's Dad."

"Ah." Not for a lack of trying, Spencer's dad is not someone I've ever gotten along with, at all. I tried, but for some reason, the fact Spencer wanted to step away and take time off from his career a few years ago meant I forced him to do it. Mr. Stoll decided my influence must have been the driving factor behind the decision, because why else would he want to take time off and essentially walk away from the bright lights of Hollywood for a little bit? Surely couldn't be because he wanted some sanity and space from a career without much time off that was driving him to the edge, but try telling Mr. Stoll that.

Spencer shifts his weight from one foot to the other. "Just a reminder for that interview I need to do soon."

Something in the furrow of his brow tells me there's more going on. I slip my hand into his and pull him so he's closer to me. "Are you okay?"

"I am." Forcing a smile, he squeezes my hand before pulling it away, but it's too late. My gut tells me there's more underneath the surface here than he's letting me see.

He looks at his watch. "Since you're taking Barney for a walk, I'll head back to the room so I can do this interview."

Pulling the key out of my pocket, I place it in the palm of his hand, my fingers lingering on his for a moment as I wait for him to look at me. He finally drags his eyes up to meet mine, and we stand like this for a brief moment. He watches me as I try to read him based on the way he looks at me. His eyes swirl as if he's been busted, but there's a caution sign that's hanging there now, too.

"Hope it goes well," I say as Barney pulls on the leash, forcing me to turn away. I go about ten paces, then turn around, half-expecting Spencer to be there watching me. Thankfully, he is.

And I like it.

FIFTEEN

Spencer

There's a tap-tap-tapping on my left shoulder, accompanied by the tinkling sound of metal. "Pass the potatoes, please."

Sitting at the long communal table, shoulder to shoulder with perfect strangers, is not how I pictured my time with Amelia on this trip. Never mind that I'm trying to woo her back into my arms. But, when I see the smile on her face and the light sparkling in her eyes as she sits amongst these complete strangers who have taken us in for the night, laughing and talking, there's no denying she's in her element.

"Here." Swiping the large dish in front of me, I pass the potatoes to the woman who tapped my shoulder, who I think said her name was Nell.

"Thanks," she purrs, taking the dish from my hands, the silver bracelets lining her arms smacking against each other and causing a melodic sound as her fingers linger on the inside of my wrist a little too long. "So, do you come this way often?"

Trying my hardest to not snicker, I shake my head. "Just passing through."

Nell smoothes her hair back, gathering salt-and-pepper

tresses and bundling them under a hair tie made out of what looks to be Christmas lights and candy canes.

"You know," she says, leaning in closer to my ear, so only I can hear her, "I know who you are. I can keep a secret."

Normally, a conversation like this would have me trying to find a way to quietly extricate myself from the room. "Oh. Well, thank you."

"I mean, I've followed your career and all that," Nell says, her voice raspy as she sizes me up. She drags her eyes across me for a second but is quick to turn her attention back to getting potatoes on her plate, and I can't blame her. They are good. "But, back in the day, I used to wait tables at this place in Boston and I always loved it when that Mark Wahlberg would come in. Now, there's an actor."

Fighting a smile, I nod in agreement. "I concur. He's one of my favorite actors, too."

"Really?" Nell's eyes light up as she digs into a giant bag at her feet. "I have a picture of us together, want to see it?"

"Sure." I take the phone as she hands it to me, looking at the screen in front of me. One glance and I silently put my hand up and say "not it" to myself—because I'm not going to be the one to tell her that's really Matt Damon in her photo.

"That's cool," I say, handing it back and turning my attention back to my meal.

"So..." She leans in close to me and wiggles her eyebrows. "Spencer Stoll, how long are you in town for?"

"As soon as our RV is fixed," I say, inclining my head in Amelia's direction, "we'll be getting back on the road."

"Ah." The woman's eyes darken as they bounce from me to Amelia. "So you two are together, together."

Confused, I choose to ignore the assumption in this woman's voice. I'm a guest here at the end of the day. "We are together, together. She's my wife."

Nell points to my left hand. "Then why aren't you wearing a ring?"

Looking down at my left hand, my stomach seizes. I'd taken my wedding band off when we first got into the RV. I always wear it and only took it off because I don't know the RV well enough and there could be a nail sticking out. Does that sound weird? Yes, but growing up, a guy on my dad's set was wearing his wedding ring and had jumped up, trying to grab something off a top shelf. Only his ring caught on a nail no one knew was there, and...yeah. You guessed it. He's got nine fingers now.

Before I can open my mouth to answer, Amelia, who I thought was busy talking to the couple across the table from us, leans over me and pipes up.

"He doesn't need to wear one." Amelia rubs my shoulder as she tilts her head and looks at me. "It's funny though, there's a statistic out there that says men wearing a wedding band are more likely to get hit on than when they don't."

I give her a playful swipe on her arm. "You must like it that I don't wear my wedding band then, huh, snookums?"

Amelia's mouth tightens when I call her that. She pinches the end of my nose, a little harder than I think she intended. She opens her mouth, ready with a good retort I'm sure, when I'm saved by Rick's interruption.

"There they are, my weary travelers. I was looking for you two," Rick says as he saunters up to the table. "How's dinner?"

"Amazing," Amelia all but purrs.

"Hey, are my meals not good enough?" I tease.

"They're good, but this"—Amelia points to her full plate —"is culinary perfection."

"She's right." I can't argue as I point to my plate. "I can't stop eating your potatoes; they're addictive."

"Glad you're enjoying the chow." Rick's brow creases as

he kneels beside us and drops his voice. "Look, I've got some kind of good but also kind of bad news. My buddy found the issue—looks like your battery has gone bad—so it could happen again on your way home."

"That's great," Amelia chirps as she claps her hands together. "And a relief."

"Well, the thing is, he can fix it, but he's had to order one in and it won't be here until tomorrow."

"That's fine." I look at Amelia. "So we should be able to get back on the road tomorrow, no worries."

"No worries," she said, pushing her chair back. "Fingers crossed."

Rick takes a moment to look at each of us before standing again. "I'm just glad that it looks like tomorrow is when it'll all happen. We had room for you tonight, but I'm not sure if we will tomorrow. It starts getting tight around here." He leans in like taking Amelia into his confidence. "That's the first night for our nativity scene. We get busy."

"Thank you again, Rick, so, so much for your hospitality." She turns to me and points over her shoulder. "It's getting dark out; want to go for a walk with me before heading back to the room?"

"Great idea!" Rick all but erupts with enthusiasm, shoving his Santa hat back as it's starting to slide off the side of his head. He looks at me pointedly. "Take her through the neighborhood that's closest to the campground. They have the best Christmas lights and decorations on that street. You'll go right out of Hubert Drive." His eyes light up as he starts to walk away. "It's a magical walk, you'll see."

We're out the door and crossing the parking lot, making our way down the driveway in the direction Rick had pointed. I take this time to sneak a look at Amelia, wondering why it is that after all these years she can make me feel like we're going on our first date again. When I see the perfect opportunity, I grab her hand and thread my fingers through hers, pulling her close to me so we can walk in sync.

As we turn the corner onto Hubert Drive, a wave of child-like wonder washes over me. The entire neighborhood is a winter wonderland, without the snow. Christmas lights shimmer while decorations sparkle like a million stars against the inky night sky. The festive spirit is palpable in the crisp, cold air, and I can't help but smile as I take in the sight.

Every house on the block should win the title of "Most Festive," as they're all nothing short of spectacular. From the rooftop Santas to the glowing animatronic reindeer scattered on various lawns, it feels like we've stumbled into a holiday-themed fairy tale. Icy garlands adorned with twinkling white lights frame various porches, and the chimneys are even crowned with full wreaths, some made of fresh greenery, and adorned with giant crimson ribbons.

We stop still, standing side by side to take in the sight before us. There's a scent in the air surrounding us of wood-burning fires mixed with the faint aroma of hot cocoa, all swirling together, making me feel as though I'd stepped onto the set of a Hallmark movie. Looking around us, I can't help but think that this is what the holiday season is all about—a shared sense of joy and togetherness, where even a simple neighborhood can be transformed into a magical wonderland of Christmas cheer.

Amelia lets go of my hand to take a few photos on her phone, turning to me and smiling with pure wonderment on her features. "Do you think this is what Candy Cane is like?"

Candy Cane Lane. Sweetkiss Creek. She pulls me out of my reverie, reminding me of my mission and why I'm here.

"I hope so," I say, shoving my hands in my pockets. "You know, I hope we get to see it. Together."

Amelia freezes, cocking her head to one side and looking at

me, her features soft. "I always hoped we would, too, Spencer."

Shaking my head, I shift my weight from one foot to the other. "I don't know if I can even remember why we spent the last year apart right now."

"Spencer. That's not funny." The softness is gone when I look at her, replaced by one stone-cold Amelia Stoll, who stands in front of me with her arms threaded tight in front of her.

"Look at us, Amelia." Surely I'm not the only one who is feeling this way. "I don't want to keep my hands off of you, and seeing you, I'm flooded with memories of the good things in my life, like why we're together. I'm here and in front of you because I need this, 'Melia. I want to make it work."

"Okay, then," she says, stepping toward me and grabbing my left hand and lifting it up so we can both see the empty ring finger. "Then where is it?"

"It's in the RV, I swear."

"You know, if this was the only time, I may let it slide. Or if you'd told me when we got married or at some point that the ring bugs you, so you take it off." She holds up her hand, showing me her left one. "Even though I've been spitting tacks furious with you the last year, I've kept this on. It's a reminder to me that there is someone out there who I love with all my heart that I'm bonded to, because I want to be."

"So you *are* still in love with me?" I ask, my voice hopeful.

"Not the point." Dropping my hand like a cinder block, she wags a finger in the air. "Do you know how many times I, or one of my friends, picked up on the fact you weren't wearing a wedding band over the last year? You've been in magazines, done interviews, and of course, there's the online gossip websites."

A sinking feeling hits the pit of my stomach. I had taken the ring off at various times, and I still do, but have I not worn it so often that Amelia and her friends would notice? I open my mouth to protest, but she holds a hand up in the air.

"Don't worry, I stood up for you." She flashes her hand in the air, her voice beginning to rise. "We're still married, after all."

"How?"

She shrugs. "I told them you break out sometimes from it, so you take it off when you get a rash. A big, sticky, itchy rash."

People around us slow down as her volume goes up, taking notice of the couple arguing on the side of the road. Easy enough to do—I think we're the only pair fighting as we stand on the edge of Santa's Happiest Place on the East Coast.

"To top it off, it was my time." Amelia's wound up now. "Me, Spencer. *Me*. I stepped back and helped lift you, like a lot of women before me have done with the men in their lives. I'm not taking the credit, but I sacrificed things I wanted to do so we could put energy into *your* career. Two of the things we agreed to talk about after we settled was putting energy behind my business ideas and starting a family."

There's the cross kick to my stomach I've been waiting for. And folks, I can't argue with this woman on this one. She's right. But I've never owned up to my part.

"I know and I'm sorry," I begin, putting my hands out to try and envelope her in my embrace, but she sidesteps the advance. "When it comes to starting a family, I wasn't sure if I was ready..."

"I couldn't have been clearer. And you had even said to me you couldn't wait for us to have a baby. You waxed poetic about when it happened how you'd be taking care of me, of us, so we could be a strong family unit. But, you left. You chose Los Angeles as soon as it came knocking again." She shakes her head at me, hurt flashing in her eyes and reflecting back at me like a mirror. I did this. "I hesitate to say you also chose your dad over our marriage, but in a way..."

I shake my head from side to side vehemently. "That's not fair."

"What's not fair is that your dad hasn't liked me since day one," she counters, waving her arms around. "You know what? I really can't recall you doing much about it. Ever. He's your dad, Spencer. He's never been welcoming to me and finds a way to blame me for your career decisions. Do you even try to stick up for me with that man?"

"Amelia..." I try reaching out again, but she shakes her head as she takes two steps back.

"No." She looks at the neighborhood beyond me, the twinkling lights reflecting in the irritated pools of her eyes, and she throws her hands in the air. "You can't even say that you defend me to your father, Spencer. When we got married, we said it was us against the world, and we'd always keep us tight. That we'd always make sure we came back to center, together, no matter what the world threw our way." She looks me up and down, disappointment flooding her features. "And look at you. Look at what your choices have done."

It stings, the truth. "I can fix this Amelia, but you have to let me."

"Not today." She starts walking back the way we came. "I'm going back to Rick's."

I know this side of her, and she needs time to think. Or at least time for me to steer clear of her so she can breathe. When we get back to the room, I'll close the door and see how her mood is. Hopefully it's a bridge I can cross again with her, if she's ready.

When we reach the entrance to Rick's, I reach out for her hand, but it's too late. Amelia's bridge has been pulled up and the gate to the castle is closed. She shoves her hands in her jacket pockets and nods her head toward the reception office.

"I'm going to pop in and ask about a rollaway bed for you. I think they close soon, so I'll meet you back in the room."

I watch as she swings the door open, closing it quietly behind her, and finding myself wishing she had slammed that sucker. A calm and upset Amelia scares me more than one who flings her emotions around a little freer. A calm and upset Amelia is more strategic and set in her ways.

In one day, I've managed to fall in and then get right back out of Amelia's good graces. Walking back to our room, my stomach rises and falls in anticipation, mad at the choices I've made.

Leaving me to wonder if I'm frozen out forever or will I have a chance to fix what I've broken?

SIXTEEN

Amelia

"You shared a bed with him, then kicked him back out of it?"

"When you put it like that, I sound crazy." I'm so grateful at this moment that we have the power of video calls. On the screen in front of me, my three besties sit huddled in Dylan's kitchen, talking me off the ledge. "I don't know, it's like we're talking things out kind of, but circling the elephants in the room."

"That's a big room." Etta chuckles as Riley smacks her arm. "Ow!"

Riley wags a finger in the air. "There's no joking during affairs of the heart."

"Where is he now?" Dylan asks, rolling her eyes and pushing the other two out of the way so she can be in the middle.

I hold up the note I'd found on the bedside table. "Went for a run. I didn't know he started running. I'm wondering if there's other things I don't know, too."

"You guys were pretty much separated for a year; it's a long time," Etta reminds me, not that I needed it.

"Just go with the flow," Dylan chimes in. "You're going to figure things out. It just may take a little more time than you want."

A lump forms in my throat as a horrible thought enters my mind. "What if the answer is to be apart?"

"You're the one who served him with the divor—" Riley begins, but Etta and Dylan stop her with a smack each. "Ow!"

"It doesn't matter who did what, what matters is you're talking, right?" Etta, a voice of reason, turns the phone so I can see her better. "If the answer is to be apart, then you'll come to it naturally, but you need to talk about the hard things first."

I'm letting her words sink in when there's a knock at the door. Pulling the curtain back, I find Spencer standing there in his running gear, looking about as energetic as I feel. He holds up a couple of coffee cups and smiles sheepishly.

I let the curtain fall back in place as I pull the phone back up to my face. "Hey, he's back."

My three besties blow kisses and start waving goodbye.

"Hey," Dylan says before disconnecting, "if you need me, any of us, call."

Putting my phone down, I take a breath and open the door before crawling back into bed.

"Here." Spencer enters the room and puts a coffee on the table next to me. "I've got good news and bad news. Which do you want first?"

Taking a sip, I shrug a shoulder. "I guess the bad."

"Rick stopped me when I was getting our coffee. His friend called, and the RV is going to take another day."

My head dips. Not the news I was hoping to hear.

"Well, you can't win them all. At least we have a roof over our heads"—I nod to his rollaway bed on the other side of the room—"and we have beds to sleep on."

Spencer ignores my dig. "Yeah, not done with the bad news. You might remember Rick said yesterday this room was only available for one night. Someone's arriving later today and needs to check in, so we have to vacate while he's trying to figure out where we can stay."

"It gets better and better," I mumble with all the sarcasm I can muster.

There's another knock on the door. Spencer's still standing beside it, so he flings the door open, revealing Rick, holding his still-dirty Santa hat tight in his hands.

"Hey, man," he says to Spencer before looking in and seeing me in bed. "Morning, Amelia. Sorry about this, but there's a lot going on. I checked all of our reservations and the schedule and, unfortunately, we don't have any space in our cabins or in the motel now."

"You're joking!" Shaking my head, I fight the maniacal laughter building inside. "So, on the same night your nativity scene opens there's like...no room at the inn?"

Spencer smirks. "Good one."

Holding my coffee in the air, I toast it his way. "Thanks."

Rick ignores us, his hands flailing with anxiety. "If you don't mind, I have a spare room in my place and am happy for you guys to crash there. There's no bed, but I can get a mattress chucked on the floor for ya?"

"Sure." Leaning back against my pillows, I make a conscientious decision to not fight anything at all today. What's it all for anyway? Plus, Rick is going out of his way if he's willing to put the Bickersons, and their dog, in his own home. "Why not?"

"Oh, good. You know, finding out this morning that Mary and Joseph broke up has not been ideal." He shakes his head. "It's a nightmare is what it is."

"You didn't mention that when I saw you earlier." Spencer's eyes light up. "You don't have anyone to play Mary and Joseph?"

"We still have Mary and her three-month-old, who is our baby Jesus in the manger. Just no Joseph."

"But is there a technicolor dreamcoat?" I throw in, my wit winning at this moment.

"You're on a roll," Spencer acknowledges while Rick holds firm and doesn't pay attention to my attempt at stand-up comedy.

"I'm worried, though, because due to the amount of tears that have flowed, apparently her eyes are almost swollen shut." Rick looks my way knowingly. "Can't have a Mary who looks like she's been punched, can we?" He stops, suddenly eyeing Spencer with glee. "Wait a second. Would you mind stepping in for our Joseph? I know it's not what you're used to as far as fancy acting gigs, but it would be so cool to have you."

"Huh?" Spencer's eyes widen as they rock to mine. "Surely, it can't be a good idea..."

"What else are you going to do tonight while we wait for the motorhome to be fixed?" I wave a hand in the air. "Go ahead. It'll be fun."

Spencer shrugs. "Fine. If she says I can do it, then I'm in."

"You're the best. Everyone will be so excited we have a Joseph again!" He looks at his watch. "I need to go let the team know we're sorted and to keep it quiet that we have a celebrity in our midst. See you at the manger...if you don't know where it is, just follow the star."

Like the whirlwind he is, Rick moves swiftly and with a sense of urgency through the door and is gone as fast as he'd arrived.

Leaving us alone.

With each other.

Spencer lets out a giant breath of air as he plops on the end of my bed. "We really need to talk."

Sitting up, I smooth my hair back and wish I would have

put a bra on. I feel like I need all the support I can get right now. "We do."

"Let's start with my dad. But first..." Spencer leans into his suitcase and pulls out a plastic bag full of Christmas cookies. "Diane made these for me to bring along. She says they bring peace."

He puts the bag of cookies on the comforter, sliding them my way. Staring at the bag, I think about putting them away until after breakfast, but deciding that's a terrible idea, I shove my hand in the bag and pull a few out, throwing one in my mouth for good measure.

"These really are good cookies." I groan, chewing slowly so I can enjoy every single bite.

"Right?" Spencer takes a bite of one as well, holding it in his hand and inspecting it. "I'd love to know what she uses. Maybe I can send a bag to my dad and instigate a conversation with him, too."

Grabbing the bag, I move it over to the bedside table and busy myself smoothing down the sheets. "You need to stand up for yourself, Spencer, and what you want when it comes to him. And maybe it's not having your dad as your manager, or if he's going to be one, he needs to listen to you."

"I've tried to talk to him, but he changes the subject or finds a way to avoid the thing I want to talk about."

Still chewing, I nod. "Because if he doesn't hear you, he doesn't have to do what you want. Look, he can be a good manager, but he's too close to you. He's inserted himself in a way that crosses a boundary right into our marriage."

I watch his face for his reaction. These are things I want to say, that I need to say, but they're about his father. And that's something I need to be careful of because it's his blood. And I never want to come in between that; I just want to find a way where we can co-exist.

"I know you're right, it's just he's my dad." Spencer hangs

his head. "When Mom left because he couldn't find work, he felt like a loser for years. He came back to life when I showed an interest in acting, and when I started getting work, it was like he lit up from the inside. I thought working together was a good thing. He's got experience and it keeps him busy."

"But, he's not supposed to manage your marriage." Treading lightly, I reach out and touch his arm. "I know you feel pulled between two worlds with us sometimes; there's your dad and your history with him, and there's me and the future you're creating. I'm not asking for you to throw the past away, not at all. I want to find a way that it can all blend. But some of this is up to you and your dad, and I'm not in it."

As if on cue, his phone rings. I half expect it to be his father, in a *Field of Dreams* "speak of it and it will come" kind of way, but judging by the scowl darkening Spencer's features, it isn't.

"What's wrong?"

"It's Bex." He sighs, handing the phone to me. "It's better if you read it than I tell you."

When he hands me the phone, there's a web page open with the headline "Spencer Scrooge or Scrooge Stoll: Pick the nickname." Confused, I scroll down the page. As I read the article, a wave of shock reverberates right to my core when a photo taken of the two of us last night as we argued on the side of the road next to the animatronic Rudolph lands in front of me.

"No way." I toss the phone onto the bed. "That's on HollywoodHeadline.com?"

"And apparently also on *TMZ*, *Page Six*, and my dad's radar." He shakes his head. "Great. And I have another phone interview to do in a few hours."

"It'll be fine. If they ask about it, just say we were having a heated discussion about who was going to put the Christmas lights on the tree this year. Everyone fights about that, right?"

"Or…" Spencer turns in his seat, facing me. "I could tell them the truth."

Tilting my head to one side, I wonder where this is going. "What's that?"

He reaches out and takes both of my hands in his. "That I'm in the middle of trying to win my wife back and seem to be messing up every turn I make."

"Oh." Staring at our hands, I watch as his thumbs caress the inside of my wrists, sliding along that vulnerable space and sending a sensation of electricity up my spine. Even after all of these years, and all of this water under the bridge, Spencer Stoll can still make me light up.

"I mean it, and if I have to stand in front of you every day until I get a yes, I'm going to beg you for another chance."

"It's not that I don't want to give you another chance. We have a lot of baggage we've collected this past year, and a lot of promises made that weren't kept."

Spencer's phone cuts the air again, surprising us both. Glancing at the screen, his scowl is back— the one he reserves for his dad. He taps a button silencing it and turns back to me.

"No, Spencer." Using my hand, I indicate where he's placed the phone on the bed between us. "Call him back and talk to him. Reassure him that you can fix this during your interview."

Spencer shakes his head as he points to me and then to himself. "This is what's important right now."

"And," I say, reaching up and taking his hands in mine, "we both know you won't be able to think straight because he'll keep calling until you talk to him."

Seeing the tiny wave of panic flashing in his eyes, I realize it's not his father's reassurance he's looking for right now.

It's mine.

"Hey." Standing, I pull him up with me and wrap my arms around his neck. "I'm not going anywhere. In case you've forgotten, our transportation won't be ready until tomorrow, and you and I are sharing yet another room tonight. So, it's pretty much a sure thing at this point that we'll have more time to talk. We just need to get your head in the game for today. You've got an interview and an important role to play tonight, okay?"

He wraps his arms around me as he hugs me close. "Promise we'll keep talking?"

"Promise." I pull away, grab my coffee, and head to the bathroom for a shower. "Let's get a move on. Joseph can't be late."

SEVENTEEN

Spencer

Standing outside the door to our motel room, I'm finding it an interesting juxtaposition to be surrounded by the most beautiful scenery with trees all around us like a natural canopy overhead, Christmas music playing on speakers, and, in the two minutes I've been outside, I've waved to at least five people.

Yet, on the phone that's pressed to my ear, you'd think there's a storm on its way and we need to batten down the hatches, tout de suite.

"Do you realize the amount of stress you're putting me under with these social media posts and all of these rumors spinning?" My father's words slam against my ear, his voice tight. It'll never cease to amaze me how he can take a situation someone else is in—and I do mean anyone—and make it about himself.

"Don't make this out to be more than it is." I sigh, pulling my jacket a little tighter around me and tucking my scarf in around my neck. I'm still wondering how someone could snap that photo from last night, but I also realize they were probably paid really well for it. Well, happy holidays to them. I hope they get nothing but coal in their stocking this year.

"I don't have to, Spencer. It's in the gossip columns, being talked about on the entertainment shows. Photos of a celebrity who is arguing with his wife in public? Those are the snapshots that get the rumor mill turning." My father is quiet for a brief moment. "How are things with the two of you, anyway?"

If anyone else had asked me this, I'd probably be touched. Like they really care and want to know how things are. But he's almost robotic when he asks, as if it's something he *has* to do. Like there's a checklist in front of him that says "Ask son about relationship" and a box next to it he can tick. His lack of enthusiasm about my marriage is but one of the many reasons Amelia and I had run off and eloped instead of throwing a big wedding.

"We're trying to push through something right now, if I'm being honest." Hearing scratching, I look down to see Barney at the window to our room. He's standing on his hind legs, pawing at the glass and looking out into the yard. Knowing he wants to come out with me, I crack the door open and motion to Amelia so she knows I have him, then watch him fly out the door and race into the yard to run around.

"Well, maybe you need to ask yourself the hard questions now. Like, is this marriage worth it?"

My jaw goes slack as I hear what he says. No. I must have heard wrong. "Is my marriage worth it?"

"Yes." His voice is matter-of-fact. "Sometimes you just know that it's better to take care of yourself and only yourself, instead of taking the risk and having someone else pull you down."

The man may be my father, but I've never said he was a normal one. This isn't the kind of talk I'd expect from a man who wants to pass on words of wisdom to his son, but when I think about his track record, then it makes sense...to him. Doesn't mean it has to make sense to me.

"Dad, I know you think I should be back on the West Coast, and you've made it clear you think I should be alone, but that's what *you* want. Not what I want." Movement through the window catches my eye. Peeking inside, I spy Amelia packing our things for our move to yet another room.

It's at this very moment that I realize it's what she's always done for me since we met: packed to move our things, for me. Taking care of me while I do...what exactly? Make choices for my career. For what I wanted. For what my dad wanted. If I got a film, she was the one organizing everything, from where we'd live to setting up the house when we got there, taking care of our bills and helping me with keeping my sanity, all while juggling her own work and, in some cases, running a household back in Los Angeles, too. It's not like this life has been easy on her.

"It's for you that I want these things. You're lucky, Spencer. You have a dad who has experience in this industry who can help guide you, you know."

I want to scream how it's a blessing and a curse, but I can't. At the end of the day, this man is still my father and I want to respect him. I want to have a relationship with him. He's flawed, but he's all I've got.

Then there's Amelia. And I want her to respect me, and the only way to make good with her is to put my foot down.

"You're right, I am lucky, but sometimes you don't see the whole picture and that's a problem—" I begin, but I'm interrupted.

"Considering I'm holding *Page Six* in my hands right now, I think it's fair to say I'm seeing the picture quite clearly."

The sight of Rick jogging over to me is the most welcome sight in the world. Am I thinking of chickening out of this chat? Not at all, but I can't be an angry Joseph for the nativity scene, either. I hold up my finger asking him to wait a second so I can get off the phone.

"I think once you get back to your inn in Sweetkiss Creek, we should have a Zoom with your team and talk about how to de-escalate your press," my father grunts in my ear. "I'm sure the studio's public relations team will have a crisis plan we can use."

Now he's being ridiculous. "We're not going to bother anyone this close to Christmas with this. I'm sure it can wait. This kind of thing can blow over in a news cycle or two if we wait long enough...anyway, I have to go. Can we—"

"You really should think about how we can turn this around, Spencer. Sexy Spencer is one thing, Scroogey Spencer is another."

"The fact the words 'sexy Spencer' came out of your mouth is enough to make me want to throw up a little bit." In front of me, and only hearing half the convo, Rick grins. "I'll call you and we'll discuss all of this further once I'm back in Sweetkiss Creek."

Hitting end on a call never felt so good. Looking up, I find Rick watching me with amusement.

"Must be hard being sexy Spencer," he teases. "I like to think of myself as radical Rick."

I shove the phone back in my pocket and point to the large box in Rick's hands. "Do you need help with that thing?"

"Nah." He holds it in the air. "It's for you. It's Joseph's clothes and no, it's not a technicolor dreamcoat before your wife asks." He rolls his eyes playfully. "I was going to put it in my spare room so it's there for you to change into when Amelia called the desk and said you're all packed. So I'm here to walk you guys to my place."

Feeling heat against my leg, I look down to find Barney back from his run and now leaning against me, panting and watching us as the door behind me creaks open.

"Good timing," Amelia sings, putting our two suitcases out on the porch as she looks at her watch. "Did you say Spencer needs to be ready for this scene by 3 p.m.?"

Rick nods. "Indeed. The local paper is coming out to take pictures, then we'll do three different showings, all on the hour. One at three, another at four, and the last one at five."

Reaching down, I pick up the two suitcases and nod my head. "Let's go break a leg."

"She broke her leg?"

We hadn't been inside Rick's small two-bedroom cabin with him for more than twenty minutes before he got a phone call that flipped his cheery demeanor upside down.

His mobile phone pressed against his ear, Rick vacillates between nodding his head and shaking it, every now and then grunting incoherently. When he finally hangs up, he looks defeated.

"Everything okay?" I feel like Captain Obvious, a theory that is proven correct when Amelia kicks me under the table.

"Brittany, our Mary, slipped and fell on some black ice in town. Poor thing, she managed to break her leg of all things." Narrowing his eyes, he looks my way. "It's like you're a sorcerer."

I toss my hands in the air. "Break a leg is a saying in show business; it doesn't mean to literally break your leg."

Rick's eyes widen as he paces the small space. "This whole thing is falling apart before it starts."

Sitting at the kitchen table, watching Rick pace, Amelia clears her throat. "If you need a Mary, I can do it."

"Look at you." I can't resist, snapping my fingers like little shotguns and pointing them at Amelia. "Pulling a Hail Mary at the last minute."

She fights her laughter while Rick spins on his heels and jumps in place. "Really?"

"Sure. But that solves one issue. The other is that you also need a baby for the manger." I watch her lips twitch as she thinks of a solution. "We could put Barney in it?"

I can't put a lid on the laughter that erupts from within as Rick's face goes white.

"No. We cannot do that, it's blasphemy. Here," he says, the stress in his voice evident as he jumps up and runs to a closet and swings the door open. "Your Mary outfit is in there. I need to go make sure the baby has arrived before the newspaper reporter gets here. I'll see you guys at the scene in an hour."

We watch as he rushes out the door, Hurricane Rick to the rescue as he gets back on his way preparing for the impending Christmas pageant. Locking my gaze with Amelia's, we both chuckle, the turn of events bringing a welcome reprieve for us both.

It seems that this little village's nativity scene is taking on a life of its own, and with a twist none of us saw coming.

EIGHTEEN

Spencer

Rick stands in front of us and casts one last look around at our scene, patting himself on the back as he does. "Oh, you all look incredible. Fabulous! I think we'll have a nice turnout this year."

He runs over to make sure Amelia and I are settled in as Mary and Joseph, but his eyes go wide with surprise when he looks in the manger to find it empty.

"What the...this is not funny. Where's Jesus?" He spins on one heel in a circle, his voice cracking. "Seriously. Where's Jesus?"

"He's here," a small voice calls out. When I turn around to see who it is, there's an elderly woman standing next to me, grinning as she holds a small lump wrapped in blankets out to me.

I point to the bundle. "What's in that?"

"That's Jesus," Amelia manages through gritted teeth as she holds her arms out. "He's swaddled in blankets."

The woman places the small baby in her arms while I watch, staring.

"He's Charlie and he's only a few months old," the

woman says as she nods across the manger. "Brittany, his mama, is over there, so if he gets restless you can bring him over to her."

"Of course," Amelia assures the woman, who I assume must be his grandmother. She turns around to face the shepherds standing behind us. "What say you, oh shepherds?"

One of the three men winces. "We're actually the Three Wise Men."

Another one of the trio snaps his fingers. "We forgot our crowns."

"And the frankincense and myrrh," another one chimes in.

"Nope, they're here." The one who mentioned the crowns leans into the cradle and takes the gifts out of it. "Tucked 'em here so we wouldn't lose 'em."

"Okay, folks, stop talking and settle in," Rick calls out as he eyes the Wise Men. "I'll go find your things, you stay here. We're about to start."

My eyes rock to Amelia, who sits watching Charlie and laughing.

"This is nothing short of amazing," Amelia giggles from her seat beside the makeshift bed.

I peek inside and am surprised to see baby Charlie smiling up at her as he wraps his hand around one of her fingers. I watch as a look I can only describe as pure joy ripples across her features and a thud hits me square in my esophagus.

"Folks, people are going to start walking by now." Rick is back and clapping his hands joyfully as he gives me and Amelia a thumbs-up. "Just stay like this, looking at the baby. We've got two more showings after this one, so"—he looks at me and winks—"break a leg!"

There's a small ruckus as a line of people I'd not been privy to seeing before begin to file past, snapping photos and taking their time to look at the beauty of the living nativity scene. I have to hand it to Rick and his team: they even have a collection of paper mâché angels hanging overhead, suspended from makeshift rafters as if blowing their horns to herald on the high. Animals of all kinds surround the manger; he's gathered at least one donkey, a mama and baby goat, a sheep, a horse, and two cows complete with stable hands to keep them calm.

As the line powers past, I hear Amelia making a soft shushing sound. When I look over, her hand is in the manger, patting Charlie's back as he wiggles and stirs. Amelia takes the knitted blanket lying on him and tucks it around him.

She looks up at me, concern in her eyes. "I think he's cold."

"Maybe Brittany will know." Looking around, I don't see Brittany or the woman who was with her anywhere nearby. A gurgling cry pulls my attention back to the wooden crib. "Do you need to hold him?"

Amelia doesn't have to be asked twice; she's bent over and pulling Charlie up and out of the small bed in no time, pressing him against her as she whispers something in his ear about sugar plums and Santa.

Watching her bounce this small human against her, something inside of me shifts. It's like there's a rockslide happening and I just can't stop it, even if I had the will and the way.

I have this feeling like someone has taken the hook end of a shepherd's staff and linked it to my belly button, locking it tight. It pulls me and it's twisting inside of me until I feel like I want to explode into a thousand sparkles, each one shimmering brighter than the other with all of the colors of the rainbow represented and lighting up the sky like a firework on a magical summer's night.

Oh, wow. This is that moment.

Standing here, looking at Amelia holding the baby, I now know without any hesitation what it is that I want—and it's her.

It's to have a family.

"Hey, there." My thoughts are interrupted as Brittany sneaks up to join us, leaning on a crutch and holding a scarf in one hand as she checks in on Charlie. "Is he being wiggly?"

Amelia chuckles as she continues to bounce him. "Is he ever. Do you want to hold him?"

"No." Brittany laughs. "He's so heavy, isn't he? And anyway, he looks really happy being right where he is."

Grinning, I slide my hand across his wee forehead, my heart seizing, and make eye contact with Amelia. "He really does, doesn't he?"

Ignorant of the moment happening in front of her, Brittany thrusts the scarf in Amelia's direction.

"Here. This is in case he starts crying again. He loves this scarf, so wrap it around him."

"That's a gorgeous scarf," Amelia compliments.

"Thanks, I made it." Brittany puffs her chest with pride, then continues. "If that doesn't work, you can sing 'Ice Ice Baby' and it totally chills him out."

"Really?" Amelia bites her lip. "Vanilla Ice makes him relax?"

Brittany shrugs. "What can I say? I used to watch him on repeats of *The Surreal Life*."

I wait until she walks away before I put my hands out to Amelia. "May I hold him?"

She cocks her head to the side, looks around, then back to me. "I guess so. Just don't go trying to convince him that he needs to take up acting."

"Har har." Amelia carefully places Charlie into my waiting arms, and it's like time around us stands still. Holding on to this small creature, I suddenly have this primal want to balance keeping this baby safe and protected. Just holding the bundle sends a warmth rushing through me.

"He likes you," she whispers, smiling and staying in character as people pass by, some pointing in our direction.

One of the women who has been studying the scene leans in and taps my arm. "Excuse me, but…" Her eyes bounce from Amelia's to mine. "I'm sorry to bother you, but you look like this actor, Spencer Stoll. It's not you…is it?"

While one hand wraps around Charlie protectively, the other hand flies to my fake beard, pressing it closer to my skin. Gotta make sure this sucker stays on.

"He gets that all the time," Amelia cuts in, leaning over and taking Charlie out of my grasp. "If I had a dollar for every time someone asked me if he was 'that actor,' I'd be rich."

"Oh." The woman looks crestfallen, shrugging a shoulder as she backs away. "Of course. Why would he be here, in the middle of nowhere, playing Joseph, right?" She cackles as she looks back at a group of friends waiting for her, and shakes her head. "Not him, girls!"

We watch as they make their way past, Amelia waiting for them to be out of sight before cracking up. Settling back on her chair, ever so gently she lays a fast asleep Charlie down in the crib.

"Look what you did," she whispers, pointing. "You got him to sleep."

Leaning her way, I peer over to watch the sleeping child, not even noticing that the Three Wise Men and the handful of shepherds standing with us had followed my lead and done the same thing.

Instead, my attention returns to Amelia, and I feel as if I'm alive for the first time, like I'm lit from within. There's a fire inside me that hasn't been there, ever. Not being with this woman has made me crazy the past year, and it's not something I ever want to do again.

Glancing at Charlie again, I say a silent thank you to the tiny man.

Because thanks to him, I finally know exactly what it is I want.

NINETEEN

Amelia

When I see the RV parked out front by the main office in the morning, I'm surprised at the mixture of emotions flooding my body. I figured I'd be elated to be leaving, but instead, I'm feeling anxious, both about leaving the safety of Rick's as well as driving this beast home for the last leg of what has been an intense and insane journey.

Looking around at the small crew gathered here to say goodbye to us, I feel a little empty. Sad to be leaving this amazing group of people, who have been so kind as to take us in. Even Nell, who glares at me from her perch outside her trailer, will be missed. I've loved looking at those bracelets of hers.

"Here." Brittany hobbles over to me and holds out three small packages. "Handmade knitted scarves for all three of you." She smiles at Barney. "Kids are kids, even if they are the four-legged kind."

Leaning over, I give her a giant hug, then point to her crutches "Make sure you text me and let me know how you're doing."

"And send pics of Charlie, too." Spencer's arm snakes around my waist as he sidles up beside me. "He's a beautiful boy and I can't wait to see what he becomes when he grows up."

"You'll come back again and visit?" Rick asks, hope in his voice. "I promise we'll make sure you have a spot."

I hold up his business card. "Hey, we have an in now for making a reservation."

"You two stepped up to help us when you didn't have to. Thank you." Rick's kind eyes well with tears. "We didn't make as much as we hoped we would for the shelter, but there's always next year."

"Maybe we can get them to come back," Brittany teases.

"Maybe," Spencer winks.

"Well, there's no getting rid of us now," Rick chortles. "Like your aunt, all of us here can feel the good in others. We see what most folks can't, because while we may have our rose-colored lenses on, we see through the crud and the baggage. We see the core, the very center of others, because if you're sitting still long enough, they show you their hand. Who they really are. You just have to watch, be patient, and know, in here"—he taps his heart—"that this will always guide you to what's right."

He steps forward and slides an envelope into my hand. "This is for you."

Staring at it, I flip it over front to back before placing it close to my heart. "From Aunt Hattie?"

He nods. "She'd be proud of you, you know."

"I hope so," I whisper, leaning in to give him a hug. "Thank you."

"Thank you," he says, his gruff tone a direct opposite to the tears I see in his eyes.

While Spencer says goodbye to a few other people, I slip around to the other side of the motorhome to get Barney settled in and make sure we're ready to go. I'm surprised when I get around to the door and find a man holding a cell phone in his hands, taking pictures and peeking in the windows.

An icy blast rips through my veins. "Can I help you?"

"Oh, hi." Startled, the man turns to face me. I know we've only been here for a couple of days, but I feel like I know the faces of the folks who are staying here, and this is one face that doesn't feel familiar. "I'm actually looking for the owner of this vehicle."

"You've found her." I shift my weight from one foot to the other, my instincts going off like Spidey senses.

"'Remember this face, because you're gonna see it again and again in your dreams,'" he half-spits, grinning at me wildly.

"Um..." I begin backing up, feeling a cloud of threat hanging in the air. "I think you may be looking for someone else."

"No, Amelia. I'm looking for you guys." He holds his phone up in front of him, steadying it, which makes me think he could be videoing our interaction. "Mostly Spencer, though. 'Cause a man's gotta do what a man's gotta do!'" Cocking his head to one side, he looks at me in disbelief. "Don't you recognize that quote? I feel like I'm doing my best impersonation here."

Alarm bells ring as his words slam into my stomach like a thousand kicks. "I'm sorry, I don't know that one."

"Oh." He keeps the phone trained on me, stepping closer. "They're quotes from Spencer's film, *Looking Glass*. How can you not know that?"

Shaking my head apologetically, I fight to calm my anxiety as my nerves begin to flare. I've been cornered by frenzied fans before. There's a fine line here in chatting with people who are genuinely interested in you and who you are, but there is another side to it. Like the time we were in London on the train during rush hour. We were there for a film Spencer was doing and had offered to take the director's nine-year-old daughter with us for a trip to the museum. Someone on the train recognized Spencer and she'd started screaming in the middle of the car we were in. Once we managed to calm her, she started crying. Even getting Spencer's autograph didn't do much to soothe the excited fan—the downside to the Spencer Effect. It had rattled me, scared the little girl, and meant we had to hop off the train ten stops earlier than planned. Not fun at all.

"I'm not the one who has to learn the scripts for the movies; it's Spencer." I take a slow step back toward the way I came.

"Well, I know you're Spencer Stoll's estranged wife." He grins a little enthusiastically, lowering his phone. "Come on. Give me the inside info so I can be the one to share it on social media––is the divorce happening?"

I'm sure my face registers shock and awe as he pulls the phone back up to a worthy height and takes aim. Where there was fear a moment ago, now I'm mad. Eyeing the door to the motorhome, I find myself wishing I was safe inside it.

"You need to leave, now." As he steps closer, I pull my keys out of my jacket pocket, thinking I can use them to hold him back (yeah, right), but thanks to shaking hands, I drop the set, watching as they bounce under the RV. Great.

"Once I get to see Spencer and get an autograph, I'll be gone." He keeps the phone aimed in my direction. "Or you can tell me, my followers, and all of his fans what's going on with you two?"

"You really should go," I interrupt his diatribe and take a step back, peeking under the RV for the keys. "I need you to leave before I scream, and believe me, I can do it loud."

"I believe you." When I glance up to see what he's doing, I find him still aiming the camera my way. I swear, I'm going to grab that phone of his and shove it where the sun doesn't shine if he keeps it up. "I know you can hold your own; who do you think got those photos of you two last night and sent them into the tabloids?"

Red. I am seeing nothing but red, and it doesn't mean stop. Spotting the keys, I bend down and swipe them up, then turn around seething and point at the man's chest, waving my finger in the air.

"You're disgusting. I hope karma finds her way to your home for Christmas as you spend the money you made on our photo." I all but spit my words at him, willing myself to wipe the smirk off his face, but he presses more.

He takes a step toward me, backing me into the RV, so now I have nowhere to go as he grabs my arm. "I've been following your husband for years, and if you only knew..."

Tuning him out, I rack my brain for a way to get attention, help. Realizing the keys I'm gripping can do the trick, I press on the alarm button attached to the RV key fob and grin as the horn begins blaring, cracking through the air around us.

"What. Do. You. Think. You're. Doing?"

I don't have to look around to know who that is. The bass in Spencer's voice tells me he's teetering on the edge. Spinning around anyway, I see rage flashing across his features, and even in my most frightened state, I know that a photo of him standing up for me could be blown out of proportion. In so many ways.

The man freezes for a second, but he lets go of my arm and takes a step back as Spencer rushes our way.

The man has no time to react as Spencer steps in front of me, pushing me behind him, his hands fisting while his biceps twitch. Thrusting his chest out, he stomps the ground with his foot.

"I dare you to make one more step toward her," he growls.

"Oh, come on." The man puts his hands in the air in mock surrender. "I'm a fan, Mr. Stoll."

Spencer opens his mouth to retaliate, but he's beaten to the punch when a familiar raspy voice pipes up.

"Who do you think you are, bullying our Mary and Joseph?"

The smirk slides off the man's face as he turns around. From the other side of the motorhome, Rick has appeared as if out of thin air, with a lot of familiar faces surrounding him. I recognize the Three Wise Men, a few shepherds, Santa, and even Mrs. Claus, all standing with Rick, who is right at the front of the small crowd. They do *not* look merry and bright.

"You're surrounded." Spencer grabs my hand and threads his fingers through mine, pulling me close to him. My front is now touching his back so we're more than intertwined, we're connected. With his other hand, he reaches back and makes sure to pull me in close so my body is flush with his, as if affording me more safety.

The man shoves his phone back in his pocket as he waves his hands. "I'll go. I was just here trying to get an autograph."

"You were bullying one of our friends!" someone shouts from the throng that's gathered around us, with others chiming in as the stranger realizes he's got no way out.

Spencer's grip on my hand grows tighter as he holds his other hand out to the stranger.

"We'll let this slide," he manages, firmly, "but you need to delete that footage. Any of it and all of it."

The man shakes his head. "No way. I have followers to answer to on Instagram and TikTok."

There's a murmur and rumble as the crowd steps forward. The influencer's eyes scan the throng before he turns back to Spencer, defeated.

"Fine," he grumbles.

Spencer snaps the phone from his outstretched hand and

starts pulling up the videos and photographs, deleting them one by one. When he's done, he hands it back, but Spencer's expression changes. Softening somewhat, but not too much.

He puts the stranger square in his sights as he wraps an arm around me. "Do you want to press charges, Amelia?"

I think about it for a moment, my anger beginning to subside. Thinking that there has to be a way we can turn this into a moment in our favor, I shake my head no. Instead, I stand on my tiptoes and whisper my idea into Spencer's ear.

When I pull away, he looks at me, his eyes rocking across me as his hands massage my arms. "Are you sure?"

Nodding, I step aside as Spencer clears his throat and faces the intruder. "You're lucky my wife isn't going to press charges against you—and don't get it twisted, she could."

The man opens his mouth as if to speak, but Spencer shuts him down. "Instead, she's asked we give you a chance. Do you want to make this better?"

The pain in our butt eyes his phone, still clutched in Spencer's fist, before looking back at us and nodding.

"Awesome." Spencer acknowledges. "Let me tell you what you're gonna do."

"I still don't see anything, Spencer."

"Keep refreshing the feed," he repeats, keeping his eyes on the road. Thankfully, because I was so shaken, he'd offered to drive, giving me time to see if the intrusive influencer had kept up his end of their deal. With HollywoodHeadline.com's website pulled up in front of me, I do as I'm told and hit refresh again, and this time I'm finally rewarded.

A tiny squeal escapes my lips. "There it is!"

In the photograph in front of me is a throng of happy people cheering next to their roughshod manger, with Rick in the middle. Grinning, I turn the screen so Spencer can get a quick glimpse.

"Did he put everything in the caption we told him to?" he asks.

I scan the copy, nodding with excitement as I read. "Sure did. He used the part we gave him about the charity Rick gives to and how they need to hit a goal so they can make sure the people in the local shelter are taken care of at this time of year. Plus, he's added a link to their Instagram bio to make it easier for people to donate." I pump a fist in the air. "Oh, that feels so good!"

I throw my hand in the air for Spencer to high-five, and he does, holding on to my hand when I try to let go.

"We do good things when we work together, Mrs. Stoll," he says with a grin.

Pulling my hand back, I take the envelope out of my lap—the one Rick had given me before we left—and hold it in the air.

Spencer eyes it before turning his eyes back to the road. "Is that the last letter?"

"I think so, unless that suitcase I still need to open has any last surprises." Flipping it over, I tear into it, pulling out a folded-up sheet of paper embossed with Aunt Hattie's initials. Casting my eyes across it, I'm a little flummoxed, but only for a second.

I'm beginning to see a pattern here.

"What's it say?" Spencer asks.

"It's not a letter as much as it is a saying, I guess." I flip the paper over to see if there's anything else written on it, but when I don't find anything, I flip it back and stare at the words.

Spencer reaches over and squeezes my knee. "Read it to me?"

Clearing my throat, I do as I'm asked. "Marriage is not

about a big beautiful wedding, or the perfect home with a white picket fence. It's not about cute kids or perfect pets. It's not about classy swanky interiors, a perfect meal, and fancy cars. Marriage is standing for love and what you believe in, it's hospital stays and struggles. It's not seeing eye to eye, but knowing that's okay and that there's freedom in spite of the dark. It's paying the bills and also having the faith that through it all, you'll come out on the other side stronger, together."

It's quiet in the cab of the RV as I finish reading and place the note in my lap. A lone tear slides down my cheek and across my jaw as Spencer's hand reaches across and envelops mine.

TWENTY

Spencer

Pulling off the highway, I stretch my neck to the right as I put on my blinker and slide the RV into a parking space. The rest stop we choose for a quick break is actually pretty busy and full, not surprising with so many people on the road wanting to be home for Christmas.

"Thanks for that," Amelia says to me as she unclips her seatbelt. "I'd like to say I'll be really quick, but"—she points to a long line creeping out the women's restroom door—"it could be a hot minute before I get back."

Pulling my phone out of my pocket, I wave it at her. "I've got a few calls to make. Take your time."

I wait until she's closed the door before I tap my phone and hit send. Before we get back to Sweetkiss Creek, there's one person I need to deal with and it needs to happen now.

My father answers on the first ring, his mood jubilant. "Well, aren't you a publicist's dream? There's some amazing footage of some charity project you took part in recently, with you dressed up as Joseph?" He chuckles in my ear conspiratorially. "Brilliant."

"It wasn't for PR, Dad." Not that he'll believe me.

"It's viral, Spence. Hollywood A-List actor appears out of nowhere to play Joseph in a nativity scene. Apparently the charity that was plugged is up to its ears in donations already and the story only went live a few hours ago." A happy sound gurgles from his throat. "I bet we get an offer from Broadway, now, too."

Hearing the news about Rick's charity makes me happy. "That's great. Rick and his little community needed the boost."

"Well, now it's time for you to ride this wave. Nothing beats momentum like more momentum, so let's keep it going." My dad clears his throat and starts to rattle off a list at me. "I've got another interview lined up with a reporter out of London, and after that, we can roll into a live feed on Christmas Eve with an entertainment channel in Australia, but before we say yes to that..."

"That's not why I called, Dad."

"Oh." He stops talking for a moment. "I mean, I guess this can wait, but I've got people who need answers now. Also, that was good you had Amelia with you in the pictures. Very good for your reputation."

"Oh, man, when did we get so far off course?" Shaking my head, my eyes rock over to where Amelia stands in line. "Amelia's in the pictures with me because she's my wife, Dad. I love her. I'm in love with her, still, after all this time. And you know what? I'm pretty lucky because I think she's still in love with me, too."

My dad breaks his silence with a cackle. "Come on, son. No one is saying we got off course, are they?"

"It's not about that. It's about the fact..." Trailing off, I search for the right words to say. "I want a father, not a manager or a business partner. And I think if we're going to make this work, we need to not work together."

"Wh-what?" he stammers. "Spencer, I'm sorry if I've done something to upset you."

"Not just me. Amelia. You've never taken my relationship with her seriously, even after we've been married for years. Most families would rally behind a member who was having marital issues, but not you. You've been kind of steering me in a direction that leads far away from my wife and from the life I was attempting to start with her."

"I'm really confused, Spencer. How is my supporting you and driving toward your goals taking you away from your life?"

Taking a breath, I calm the nerves shaking inside me. "Your actions toward Amelia aren't kind, and she's aware of it. Do you know what she did when I told her I was upset with you? She didn't encourage me to call you up and go off on you, or fire you, or cut you out of my life. She asked me what I wanted to do and told me she'd stand by my side. No matter what because you're my dad and she wants me to have a relationship with you. But I need to know that you are willing to try, too."

"To do what?" he asks, his voice teetering on indignance.

"To get to know her. Give her a chance. Get out of your own narcissistic way and meet your daughter-in-law halfway, Dad." Sighing, I lay my head on the steering wheel. "I'm not coming back to LA. I'm staying here. I can fly to LA if I need to. I can fly anywhere I need to for that matter. If someone wants a meeting, we can set it up over Zoom."

"But..."

"Not done. You need to book a ticket to fly out here at the beginning of the year so we can all be together. As a family. And I don't know what that looks like right now, except that it starts with you getting to know Amelia. My wife. And, God willing, if she will truly take me back, the future mother of my children."

The silence on his end thumps in my ears as I take a small breath of air, filling my lungs after my soliloquy.

"Wow." He clears his throat.

"Yeah. Wow is right."

"That's a lot you just said there, Spencer. It's like you've been holding that in."

"Because I have been." Sighing, I sit back up straight. "And I shouldn't have. I owe it to Amelia to make this right, and it starts with you. Because if you can't get it together, then I'm sorry, Dad, but I'm getting another manager."

"Don't do that." His voice hushes, his tone sounding defeated. "It's not easy to have your only child hold a mirror up to you and show you how you've been acting. It took a lot for you to tell me that, and all I can say is, I will do better. I'm sorry, Spencer."

I almost can't believe my ears. "Yeah?"

"I really am. Not going to lie, it's been like getting a do-over being able to work with you on your career. You're reaching such great heights, and I just didn't want anyone to pull the rug out from under you," he says, his voice cracking. "Like your mother did to me."

"Oh, Dad," I begin, but he stops me.

"No, don't. I should be over it and not let my past get in the way." He chuckles. "I was going to get busted for being half-jealous of my son and his awesome life at some point, but now that I can admit it, maybe I can work on being more supportive instead."

Looking out the window, I scan the line for Amelia but don't see her. I don't know how much time I have left, and there's still one more phone call I have to make if I'm going to do all of this the right way.

"I love the sound of it, and I think we'll start in January. I'll book you a ticket to fly in for New Year's with us, okay, Dad?"

"And maybe we can start a little yearly tradition of our own?" His voice is hopeful.

"I'd like that. And I think Amelia would, too."

He sighs on the other end. "I have a lot of making up to do with that woman."

"You do, and I don't envy you one iota being in that position," I say with a half-laugh. "But I know that if she can see her way to forgive me, which remains to be seen, I'm sure she'll give you another chance as well."

"I'd like that, son." He's quiet for a moment before speaking again, his voice breaking. "Love you, Spencer. And I'm sorry."

"New starts, Dad." Smiling, I tap the steering wheel. "And I love you, too."

As soon as we disconnect, I reach into Amelia's purse, looking for her cell phone. I'm rewarded when I find it buried at the bottom. She's got it locked with a code, so crossing my fingers, I try our wedding date to see if it opens it, and voilà... score on the first try.

Tapping her contacts folder, I scroll through until I see the name I want pop up in front of me. Tapping the screen, I press the phone to my ear.

TWENTY-ONE

Amelia

Pulling into the driveway of the rental in Sweetkiss Creek, something in the air feels different. Glancing Spencer's way, I find him staring at me with an odd expression.

"You okay?"

"I'm not sure." Unbuckling his seatbelt, he turns in his seat to face me. "I can't put my finger on it, like I forgot to turn something off before I left home..."

"Same." I look out the windshield at the little house, sitting empty and sadly under-decorated. It's un-Christmas-like feel matches the mood I was in pre-road trip. "At least we made it back in one piece, though, right?"

I start gathering things we've strewn about the front of the RV like my phone, his baseball hat, a pile of maps, our empty soda cans and putting it all in one bag. By all rights and means I should move my body out of the seat and start unpacking, but I don't want to yet.

Spencer's eyes rock over to where his car sits in the drive-way. "Do you know when you're going to look to see what's in the suitcase?"

"I was going to do it once I got inside, but"—I shoot him a sly grin—"it's been our adventure. Wanna open it together now?"

Spencer grins. "You bet I do. Is it in the back?"

"It's strapped down to the bed," I call over my shoulder as I walk to the back of the RV with Barney prancing his way ahead of me.

Undoing its tether, I step back as Spencer hoists it onto the bed and stands beside me. "The note Aunt Hattie left for this one was that you'd know when to open it, right?"

Nodding, I pull my hair back into a low ponytail and eye the suitcase. "No time like the present, I guess."

Taking that as his orders to move, Spencer leans forward and unzips the bag, pulling the top back and tilting it open so we can inspect the contents it's been keeping safe inside.

The first thing to catch my eye is a small homemade nativity scene that looks like it's seen some mileage. It's complete with popsicle sticks as the manger and wooden clothespins as Mary and Joseph.

"I made this!" I giggle, holding it up for Spencer to see. "Self-fulfilling prophecy there, huh?"

"That's cool," he says, taking it from me. "How come it's the first time I'm seeing it?"

"I gave it to Aunt Hattie for Christmas one year." I place it to the side and dig into the bag, pulling out a small cardboard box. Opening its lid, I'm surprised to find several small ornaments that look like stars made of yarn, cookie cutters with bows, and even pieces of cardboard decorated with glitter and sparkles and cut into shapes like snow globes complete with white glitter as snow, Christmas trees, ornaments, candy canes, and the like.

Turning one over in my hands, I run my finger along something written on the back of one of the cardboard ornaments as a fleeting memory comes to the forefront of my mind.

"I helped her make these." Pulling them all out, I lay them on the bed for Spencer to see.

"Nice globes," he teases, hip checking me as he points to the snow globes and waves a hand over the cardboard section of the holiday collection. "Explain these to me. I can see they're in the shapes of Christmas trees and candy canes, but why are there stick people drawn on some of them?"

Picking one up, I turn it over in my hands. It's the one shaped like a Christmas tree and, in the very middle, are four stick figures, one wearing a crudely drawn Santa hat. The outside rim is decorated with green ribbon and somehow I'd managed to glue a tiny golden star to the top of the tree.

"These folks," I say, pointing to the stick people, "are my family."

Spencer tilts his head to one side. "Your parents, you, and your sister?"

"No. The family I wanted to have when I 'grew up and got married.'" Laughing, I gently place it back in the box, pulling out an empty ice cream tub.

"Hope that was empty when it went in," Spencer jokes, inclining his head toward the ice cream container as he picks up the Christmas tree ornament again to look at it closer.

"Har, har." Opening the tub's lid, my heart skips a beat when I see Aunt Hattie's angel topper sitting inside, nestled on top of a pillow-like pile of satin fabric. "I wondered what happened to this! I was with her the day she bought it, in fact, I picked it out."

I turn to Spencer, holding out the angel to show him, only to find him still staring thoughtfully at the Christmas tree ornament. Keeping it cradled safely in the palm of his hand, he slams his eyes into mine.

"This was your dream when you were a little girl?"

I nod. "I'm pretty sure I wanted a horse, too."

He shakes his head. "But the family part...do you still want to have that?"

"I do." I put the angel down and stare over his shoulder at the ornament in his hand. "But..."

How do I tell him that I know what I want, that it's taken me going on this trip with him to see what it is that I really and truly need to have in my life? My tummy does anxious flips back and forth, and I start fiddling with my fingernails, running the tips of my fingers over their sharpest parts and forcing myself to stay in the moment.

I'm about to open my mouth when R2D2 starts a series of beeps that make me think the Imperial Army must be closing in. I cross the RV back to the front of the cab to grab my phone, relieved when I look at the screen to see it's only Bex.

"Hey," I call out, holding it up for Spencer to see. "It's Bex. She's trying to get a hold of you. Says we need to look at your dad's latest TikTok?"

Still holding the ornament, Spencer swipes his phone from his back pocket and opens the app. In a few seconds, the sound of his dad's voice fills our small space. I walk back over, peeking over his shoulder to see what it's about.

Spencer's dad isn't the kind of person who uses TikTok a lot. Spencer says he checks it mostly for seeing what people are saying about the movies he does or keeping tabs on Spencer's fan base. But his dad ended up with a huge number of followers when it clicked for people that he's *the* Spencer Stoll's father.

His dad sits in front of a Christmas tree, hunched over with his elbow on his knee holding his chin up with the fist of his left hand as he talks directly to the camera. I'm half paying attention, more mesmerized by the twinkling of the lights on the tree behind him if I'm honest, but when I hear my name, my ears perk up.

"Wait—" I grab Spencer's arm. "Can you rewind that?"

Thumbing the screen, he slides it back, rewinding the video to the beginning as he hands me the phone.

"Merry Christmas, you guys, happy holidays…I don't know what to call you, TikTok'ers is that right?" He chuckles, his eyes starting to dart around with some unexpected awkwardness seeping through. "I wanted to get on here because there is someone out there who I need to say I'm sorry to."

His eyes return to the camera, staring directly into it and making me feel like he's speaking only to me.

"Amelia, I've not been fair and for that, I am sorry. You may think I'm crazy to apologize here, but I didn't want to only say sorry to you when I see you in person. I also want folks to know that I've been recalcitrant in the way I've treated you over the years. It's not a very kind way for a father-in-law to act, is it?"

"No," I find myself whispering, fighting to keep my jaw from unhinging as Spencer snakes an arm around my waist and pulls me tight to his side.

"Folks, if you're watching this, just know people make mistakes. We all do, and we can give lip service all we want, but it's our actions that matter and owning what we do. And my actions toward my own daughter-in-law have been unfair for her and unwarranted. This is the day I start changing. They say an old dog can't learn new tricks, but I don't buy into that."

His expression softens as he leans in closer to the camera. "I'm sorry, Amelia. Truly sorry. It took someone very special to both of us to get me to look in the mirror at myself, and I promise I won't stop here. My lessons are just starting. And, to anyone else, if you're watching this and you have someone in your life you need to say you're sorry to, please just go and do it now. Mend the fence and don't let things wait too long. I can only hope I haven't. Merry Christmas, everybody."

As the video loops and starts to play again, I pass the phone back to Spencer.

"Wow." My eyes wide, I meet his gaze. "You talked to him?"

"Yeah, but I didn't tell him to go that far." He wraps his other arm around my waist and pulls me in tight to his chest, kissing the top of my head. "I told him he needed to fix things, not to lay out a grand gesture, but I'm glad he did."

"And you did that for me?"

"Of course I did," he says, pulling back and craning his neck to look down at me. "Believe it or not."

A jumble of thoughts and emotions rush through my head when I remember seeing the envelope Spencer had brought with him on the trip. The envelope. The one I had arranged to have sent to him at just the right moment to push his buttons.

Untangling myself from him, I make my way back to the front of the RV, my eyes drawn to a stack of papers on the dining table. Rustling through them, I cry out in victory when I find what I'm looking for.

Opening the envelope, I slide the papers out and walk back to Spencer. The happiness reflecting across his face disappears when he sees the documents in my hand.

"Are those—?"

"The divorce papers I stupidly had sent to you in a moment of anger and frustration?" I hold them up in between us and wave them around like a floppy rag. "They sure are."

Gripping them in front of me, I clench the papers and tear them apart, ripping them into two giant chunks, throwing the pieces in the air around us. "It was pretty childish of me to do that, Spencer."

As the papers scatter on the bed and floor around us like

giant snowflakes, Spencer eyes me with what I would call playful caution. "Do you mean that?"

I nod. "I wanted your attention, for you to know I was serious about how I felt. But one thing that comes up over and over is that I want a family, right? Well..." I wave my arm around him and Barney in a giant circle. "I have one. This *is* my family. So what if it's not stick figures on an old ornament? It's mine, even if it doesn't look like I thought it would."

Cupping his face in my hands, I stand on my tiptoes and slowly brush my lips across his. "I don't want anything else but you."

Everything around us fades away as Spencer's hands clench around my waist, grabbing me and slamming me into his body as his lips slant across mine. A shiver races across my skin as his hands dance up the side of my body, his fingers doing a gentle ballet up the length of my arms, only to grow more forceful as his hands entwine themselves in my hair.

Everything inside me has waited for this moment. Nothing else matters except that we're both here, we're both willing, and we both know that we're in this for the lifetime and not for a season or a reason.

Sighing, I let a small groan escape as his lips drag across my cheek and down the side of my neck, and he places soft and slow kisses along my jawline, leading to my ear. My eyes closed, I lean into him, allowing him to show me who he is to me and remind me of the passion and heat we have when it's the simplicity of us.

His kisses come slower now, more languid. I don't want this to end, but reality is, there's an ornament of some kind pressing into my backside and I need to move it before it pierces my skin.

Giggling, I reach behind me and pull one of the yarn stars out from where it stabs my derriere, showing it to Spencer. "Star light, star bright?"

Chuckling, he swallows a groan himself as he buries his face in the side of my neck.

"I'm glad we have that suitcase full of your holiday memories." He pulls away slightly, brushing my hair back from out of my eyes as he looks into them with an intensity I've not seen before. "I want us to have our traditions, in our home, doing our thing, you know?"

Right then, the ringing of his phone pierces the air around us. Since I've pretty much just laid my heart down on the middle of railroad tracks for him, I half expect him to ignore it. Instead, he holds up one finger and leans in to kiss the tip of my nose.

"I know we're having a moment, but..." He gives me a sheepish grin and a wink. "Give me one sec."

Turning his back to me, he opens his phone to read his message, turning back to me with a look of amusement dancing on his features.

"I know the timing here isn't the best, but I need to go." He looks at his watch. "Now."

Cocking my head to the side, I narrow my eyes playfully. "You do? Like right now, right now?"

"Don't read into this," he says, sweeping me back into his arms. "I have to take care of something. Just give me a few hours. Meet me later tonight. Please?"

I nod. "Okay."

He kisses my nose. "Bring Barney."

"Okay." I laugh, giving him a playful shove toward the door.

"I'll get in touch and tell you where we'll meet." He flings the door open, leaping out of the RV and onto the driveway. "Trust me?"

Looking at him, a giddy rushing jumble of heat whooshes through me, sending a shiver of goosebumps across my flesh. After all of this time, the years we've been together, and what we've just been through, of course I trust him. With every bit of my heart and my soul. I trust and love this man. To ridiculous heights.

And I hope this ride we're on, as insane of a roller coaster it is, never ends.

"I do."

TWENTY-TWO

Spencer

"Wow, when you said you'd be able to get it together for me by tonight, I had my doubts, but you guys are fierce."

Things I'm learning about my new hometown: don't mess with the women of Sweetkiss Creek. Standing in the middle of the living room of our newly built home, which had been completely void and empty of anything about an hour prior, my heart swells with pride and anticipation.

"We're known to work miracles," Etta says as she wipes down the kitchen counter. "Although, moving someone into a house in a day with an hour's notice is a whole other situation altogether."

"Be fair," Dylan says, coming to my defense. I think I like her best out of all Amelia's Sweetkiss Creek friends. "It's not like we really moved them in here, we're just setting them up until they can coordinate the rest of the move."

When I got the idea to surprise Amelia, my gut reaction was to throw money at everything and go all out. However, I knew if I did, she would shake her head and tell me to be smarter with our money. One thing I want to do, from here on out, is to not only listen to what she says, but to also put those words into action 'cause we're a team.

A bang comes from the dining room, where Riley is busy arranging the folding card table and making sure the flower arrangement I splurged on in the center of it looks perfect.

"Yeah, I think bringing over a couple of beanbags for living room furniture and folding chairs is a far cry from moving someone in, Etta," she teases before looking my way and placing a hand on her hip. "What are you guys going to do for a bed?"

That's one thing I've already thought about. "I'm going to drag the mattress in from the RV."

Riley nods in approval as Etta's face registers slight shock.

"That would make me..." she begins.

"So happy that someone thought of you," Dylan finishes, appearing beside Etta suddenly and nudging her in the ribs with her elbow. I totally get where Etta is coming from, but yeah, I can see double dates in the future with Dylan and Reid, that's for sure.

Looking at my watch, I wave my hands toward the door. "She's going to start getting antsy. I need to text her to come meet me."

"He's right," Dylan says, clapping her hands together and shooing the other two out the door. "And I need to pick up Reid from work soon. His shift on the ambulance ends in fifteen minutes."

I knew calling Dylan for help was the way to go. I've listened to Amelia talk for months about her friends: Etta getting her wine shop started at the campground, the perfection that is the marriage of Dylan and Reid, and Riley working to claim her independence from her family as she ventures out of their protective sphere and tries to make her own way.

But I knew, when it came to what I wanted to do for

Amelia tonight, I needed to have their help. My wife deserves the grand gesture, and not just the one my own father beat me to, either.

The sound of a throat being cleared breaks my thoughts. When I turn to see who it is, I find Dylan with a huge smile plastered on her face.

"Well," she says, picking up her purse from the floor. "Looks like it's time for us to go."

The trio head out the front door, taking turns looking behind them and patting each other on the back for the work they'd done. I make a mental note to text Bex as soon as I can and get gift certificates to the closest spa for a girls' day for this group of women, and stat. They deserve it. Everyone needs to have friends like this in their lives, and I'm glad they're there for Amelia.

Dylan's the last one out the door. She stops and turns to face me, giving me a thumbs-up. "You've done good, Spencer."

She leans in and gives me a quick hug before retreating and jogging to the car to catch up with her friends.

Pulling my phone out, I text Amelia the address where she needs to meet me and then I pull a bean bag up to the window so I can watch for her and wait.

Amelia

When I pull onto Candy Cane Lane, my heart does a gleeful little dance. I can't help it, it's what happens when you see all of the houses in a row, twinkling with lights and decorated as far as the eye can see. Cars drive much slower than the usual speed limit on these nights, more of a casual scooting they adhere to because of the number of visitors walking the streets, drinking hot chocolate, buying mistletoe, and singing carols as they take in the scene.

Honestly, if Hallmark owned a neighborhood, it would one hundred percent be this one.

Turning down American Legion Drive, I scan the houses lining the street. What sold me on building our home here was when I heard about the community spirit and how alive it is, especially at Christmas. The lights are dazzling, displays that rival anything I've ever seen in the movies. It's like the neighborhood has been wrapped in a technicolor seasonal bow. Houses are themed and have been impeccably organized, and local vendors keep the entrepreneurial spirit alive as they thread through the cars selling Christmas cookies and candy canes.

A canopy of twinkling lights drapes from tree to tree, criss-crossing the streets. Some homes have even gone so far as to construct archways made of candy canes (note to self: must level up if we stay here). But me, I'm only passing by, headed to the dark lot at the end of the street that backs up onto the lake.

Surreal with a sprinkle of promise is the feeling I get pulling in the driveway. I know Spencer's here—he's the one who texted me the address—but all of the lights are off. Luckily, the amount of light emitting from the homes surrounding ours leaves the area feeling like it's midday to some degree, but I digress.

Hopping out of the car, I open the back door, releasing Barney, as I pop open the trunk to grab the suitcase. Barney circles my feet while I haul it out, plopping it on the ground beside me so I can close the trunk.

Grabbing the handle of the suitcase, I look down, expecting to see Barney still at my feet, but he's gone already.

"Barney?" When I look around, he's not in the yard. Since it is lit up like Vegas around here, I'd see him if he was running around the lawn. Cars are moving past at a steady and super slow pace, but I'm still relieved when I glance at the road and don't see him navigating his way around any vehicles.

When I turn back around to face the house, Barney's at the corner of it, half of him hidden by one of the remaining shadowed spots on the lawn.

"There you are." Still holding the suitcase, I trod across the lawn to commandeer him inside, only he's got other plans. Something catches his attention in the darkness behind the house where the property borders the lake, and he takes off.

Groaning, I jog after him. "Barney, come on! It's cold out here—"

I'm mid-step following him when, suddenly to my left, the exposed back wall of the house lights up. I stop in place, squinting in confusion, trying to understand what I'm seeing. A photograph?

As the picture in front of me begins moving, a surge of familiarity is joined by a tidal wave of emotion as reality sinks in. My eyes widen, my jaw for real unhinging. I think it almost hits the ground when I realize it's a film. Someone is using our home as the backdrop for their projector.

A scene floats on the wall in front of my eyes, showing a couple embracing in a crowded airport, stealing a kiss...and I know what this is. It's the absolute epitome of voyeurism, at least in my mind, when one participates in people-watching at an airport. Personally, I love it. Hugh Grant's voice begins to boom across the backyard and echoes around the lake while he explains his love of the arrivals area at Heathrow. My heart slams inside my chest with such force, I'm afraid my ribcage will crack.

Placing the suitcase on the ground, I put the traitorous tears that fall down my cheek out of their misery, wiping them away with the back of my hand as I swallow a lump in my throat.

There's one person, only one, in this entire world who knows how much I love watching this movie at Christmas. Every. Year.

"Hey, you." Hands snake up my arms, squeezing my shoulders from behind, and I lean my body back, pressing myself firmly against Spencer's chest. Everything inside of me sparks with an electrical current when he wraps his arms around me, my hands holding fast to his hardened biceps.

"Hey." Leaning my head up and to the left, I let my lips graze his jawline, day-old stubble tickling my mouth. "You did this for me?"

I feel his chest rise and fall as he squeezes me against him. "Yep."

Spinning me around in his arms so we're facing one another, he uses his thumb and his forefinger to tilt my chin upward.

"I wanted to tell you I'm sorry." Leaning forward, he rests his forehead against mine and keeps his eyes locked on me. "I had a lot of time to reflect while we were separated. It's frustrating that it took this long for me to figure out what was wrong, but looking back, it had to happen. So I came back here to be a stronger man for you. For us."

He pushes a few stray strands out of my eyes as his slam into mine, filled with sincerity and love. "I wasn't listening to you. I heard you say what you wanted, but I wasn't truly listening. It didn't help that I wasn't sure if I was ready to be a father—"

Opening my mouth to protest, Spencer shakes his head for me to wait as he continues. "—not that I didn't want to be one with you, but because I was scared about what kind of dad I'd end up being." He looks at me sheepishly. "You've seen who my role model was. The last thing I wanted to do was to start a family and put my baggage on someone who we planned on molding and shaping into being an adult."

"Spencer." Cupping his face in the palm of my hands, I peel myself away only so I can get a better look at him. "Why didn't you tell me?"

"I didn't realize that was what my fear was about until I was alone." He looks away, his eyes downcast. "We'd moved here and you were happy, and you were settling in so fast. I mean, look at you, I'm gone a year and I come back and you're like the town mayor."

"Oh, stop." Cocking my head to one side, I try to make him smile. "Well, maybe like a vice-mayor, 'cause you know, I've got things to do."

"Do you ever." He chuckles. "It didn't sit well with me that I was kind of a recluse when we got here, and here you were going out and making friends and opening businesses, and planning the house. It seemed like all I knew how to do was make movies. And it felt kind of hollow."

"If that's the way you felt, why go back?"

"It's what I know. I figured I'd go, work really hard, and get my career to a place where I could be one of the lucky ones who lives outside of LA and flies in for work. I needed to make sure I felt good and right in here," he says, tapping on his head, "and here," he finishes, stroking his heart.

Taking one of his hands in mine, I thread my fingers through his. "Why do you think you're scared?"

Spencer lifts a shoulder and lets it drop. "My own relationship with my father is so out of balance. I was nervous I wouldn't be able to break the cycle, but now I know I can. What really scared me was that I hadn't thought of the reality. I could lose you." He shakes his head as he wraps both arms around my waist, pulling me tight again. "There's no way I'm going to let that happen."

I watch him closely as he lifts my hand to his lips, kissing it as he keeps his eyes locked on mine. "What are you saying, Spencer Stoll?"

"What I'm saying is that I realize when I hold you, like this, we can do anything, as long as we're together. If we can drive from Florida back to Sweetkiss Creek in an RV and learn how to work together to get that thing back here, we can conquer the world, come what may." He bends down, touching his nose to mine. "Amelia, I know where home is now. It's here, in Sweetkiss Creek. With you."

I don't need to hear anything else. Throwing myself into his arms, I snake my arms around his neck and pull his mouth on top of mine, the softness of his lips as they skate across mine melting my insides in ways I didn't know they could go. My reaction is seismic as his kisses trace along my neck, flicking along my jawline. There's an awakening in my body, a physical reaction to this man that tells me he is the missing piece that I need.

There's an aching for more. More than kisses, more kisses than these, for him to sweep me into his arms and drag me inside, but instead I acquiesced as his kisses began to slow. The taste of coffee and Chapstick lingers on my lips, and it's all familiar, and it's mine.

And there's time. We've got forever.

Spencer pulls back just enough so he can peer down at me through half-closed eyes. "Do you realize that the suitcase is part of a grand design plan from your aunt?"

Snickering, I look at the piece of luggage sitting lopsided on the lawn, Barney leaning against it. "I have my theories."

"I do, too." His mouth comes down on mine, his lips lingering for a moment before he pulls away again. "Mine involves an eccentric woman who loved her niece—and handsome husband I might add—so much that when she found out from said niece there was trouble in paradise, she wanted to do what she could to try to leave you—"

"Us," I interrupt, kissing his cheek.

"*Us* something to think about. So she put together a treasure trail for our ghosts of Christmas past, present, and future."

"No way," I giggle. "Do you really think that's what she did?"

"Hear me out," Spencer says as he nods. "Christmas past: our wedding photographs which we got from her old friend, Andy. Her old friend from long ago. In the past."

"Yeah, yeah." I'll play along. "So if that's the rhyme to the riddle, then Gerry would be the ghost of Christmas present?"

"You got it." Spencer tilts his head to one side, running a finger down the side of my cheek, wet glistening in the depths of sapphire-blue eyes. "He gave us the suitcase, with all of the nostalgia and traditions that your aunt wanted to hand down to us, and it came from the man who let her get away."

"Oh." When he puts it like that, there's a small stab at my heart, but only for a moment because, folks, I already know how I want this love story to end. "That makes Rick the ghost of Christmas future, giving us the poem about marriage."

"But the one thing I still can't figure out," Spencer whispers as he nuzzles my cheek, his fingers threading my hair, "is how it is I got this lucky to get another chance with you. It's not every day you get another chance to woo the woman who you want to be the mother of your children."

Stepping back, my eyes bounced excitedly to his. "The divorce papers worked. I need to use that kind of emotional manipulation again," I say teasingly, ducking to the side as he takes a swipe at me.

"Get over here," he growls, hooking his finger through my belt loop and tugging me tight against him. "When I said I do, I meant it. I know we'll have other fights, arguments..."

"Debates," I correct, winking.

"Whatever. We're just not going to let it all pile up and

then implode around us." He kisses the top of my head. "I'm really saying it out loud for me because I'm the one who ran, you were only reacting. And I am not going to stop saying I'm sorry to you. Ever."

"No. No more looking back." Craning my neck to look him in the eye, I incline my head toward the house. "New home, new chapter. New us."

"I like that." Spencer opens his mouth to say something when a horn honks from the other side of the house.

I look over and find Barney still leaning against the suitcase, but when I look back at Spencer, he's grinning at me like the cat who ate the canary.

"Is that horn for me, too?"

He waves his hands in the direction of the sound. "Go on. What're you waiting for?"

Cracking up, I sprint to the front yard. With every step, I feel lighter and lighter as if the load of the past year is sliding off me like armor I've had on for far too long. When I round the corner, I'm once again thrown off guard and can only stop in my tracks as tears stream down my cheeks.

The RV, which wasn't in the driveway when I pulled up, is parked there now, only it's decorated with Christmas lights draped along the top of it with a wreath stuck on the door. But the best part? The words "I will love you forever" are written on the side using an exceptional combination of tinsel and fairy lights.

When I look out on the street, caught in the moving slow-as-mud traffic jam in front of our house, is one Lake Lorelei ambulance with Dylan and her husband, Reid, waving from the front seat.

Waving, I stifle my laughter. These people know how to make a girl feel extra special.

"Your friends are the best." Spinning around, I find Spencer standing and smiling at me. "Dylan offered to do that to the RV, said she did something similar for another friend one year at Christmas, and apparently that couple is living happily ever after." He shrugs. "So I thought, why not? I could use all the help I can get."

"She helped you with all of this?"

"Etta and Riley did too. They all showed up with temporary furnishings we can use for now." His cheeks flush pink. "I wanted to surprise you and have a night here. In our house. Our home."

Laughing, I toss myself in his arms, jumping up and wrapping my legs around his waist. My sudden movement takes him off balance, both of us tumbling to the ground together, laughing as we roll to a stop.

"I love you so much, Spencer." Balancing on my arm, I lean over and drag my lips across his, willing him to hold me closer.

As if he's heard my internal thoughts, Spencer's arms wrap around my middle and he holds me firmly against his body. "I love you, too. And I'm sorr—"

"Shhh. No more. Fresh start and all that." I put my hand over his mouth and nod toward the house. "So are we going inside or what?"

He takes my hand off his mouth, kissing the back of it with his lips lingering for a moment. "We are, but I need to warn you, when I say temporary furnishings, it means we have limited furniture. Like, we're going to drag the mattress in from the RV kind of limited."

Hovering my mouth above his, I can't stop the grin enveloping my face.

"It's fine." Kissing his lips, I stand up and put out my hand, taking his. "We've got this."

As we sit in the backseat of the black Lincoln Town car, it's amazing how bright it can be in here with all of the flashbulbs popping off and snapping to life outside, even with tinted windows.

"Hey," Spencer murmurs, leaning across the seat to take my hand in his as he nuzzles my earlobe. "Are you sure you're feeling up to facing this crowd tonight?"

Am I ready to step out of the peace and quiet of our tiny bubble we've been living in happily for the past few months, and back into this celebrity world of his with all the bells and whistles? Yes. Returning to Los Angeles with him for this premiere feels like coming home, but it's more like a second homecoming since Spencer doesn't live here anymore. His home is with me.

"Well," turning my body away from the door, I thread an arm around his neck and tug him close to me. We're so close that our foreheads kiss and we're nose-to-nose; I can smell the faint hint of coffee on his breath, mixed with peppermint from his mints. "A few months ago, I'd have said no way and probably thrown a few four-letter words at you, but the only thing I can say now is yes. I'm more than ready to face that," I throw my thumb over my shoulder toward the waiting throng, "with you."

"Good," he growls as he snakes an arm around my waist, pulling me tighter against his firm body. "Because there is no one else in the world I want to be here with, just you."

Dragging my eyes to meet his, I feel a wisp of hair as it falls across my face, only to be swept back by him and tucked behind my ear gently. At this moment, I say a silent thank you to my Aunt Hattie, because I know without her help...or rather, forcing the situation, we may not be here today.

The car kicks into gear, bobbling a few more feet before it comes to a stop again, and we unravel ourselves as it does. This time around, I cannot keep my hands off of him no matter what. He could be covered in mud and I all want to do is rip his clothes off and––

"We should be able to get out in the next minute or two." Spencer's watching the line of cars ahead of us. "Looks like almost everyone else has been paraded out. That means it's my turn soon."

Giggling, I'm surprised when the butterflies begin tap dancing in my tummy. I mean, it is a big night for him; the reviews are more than excellent. In fact, they're stellar and there's already a buzz about a sequel...

But what he doesn't know yet is that it's a big night for both of us.

"I love how they do the build up for these movie premieres." It's cool, the bustle of all things glitzy and sparkly and Hollywood, yet it's organized chaos at its best. People screaming his name, wanting to snap a pic with my man or wrangle him to the side for a quick autograph. But I'm the one who's going home with him tonight, folks. Tonight, tomorrow night, and all the nights into forever and beyond.

"Wait in the car, we'll let the star out when everyone is good and hyped up."

Spencer chuckles. "It's part of the machine, right? Once my co-stars are out of their cars and through the line, Dad said the PR team would give us the go ahead." Spencer winks. "He also knows that we want to be on the next plane back to Sweetkiss Creek, so he's arranged for us to get on a late morning flight tomorrow."

"Outstanding. He's coming back with us this time, isn't he?"

Have I crossed into fresh territory with my father-in-law as well? I'll just say that his visit over New Year's was successful. The moment he landed, he apologized profusely, and we both agreed to let the past stay where it needs to...behind us. And now, we start over. As a united front, because we are a family of Stolls.

"He is flying out on the same flight with us and this time he's staying for two weeks." Spencer wiggles his eyebrows. "Sick of him yet?"

"We're making up for lost time, so no, I'm not sick of him. But I will force him to go with me to play bingo at the Sweetkiss Creek Police Department fundraiser."

"And he'll have a blast." Spencer laughs as he straightens his time. "Before I forget, Bex said she'd bring Barney to us at the airport tomorrow to save us coordinating his pick up before we leave."

Did we bring our baby with us? Of course we did. As long as that dog can travel with me, he's coming. At the moment, he's with Bex's best friend snuggled up in her apartment for the night. The last photo she sent us was of Barney passed out with his favorite toys around him. My heart is full.

Peering back outside, I spot a group of people we know slinking past the throng and weaving around the paparazzi to make their way into the theater.

"Look." I tap on the window for Spencer. "They made it!"

"Wow, Etta and Zac look great!" He says as he leans across me, his breath hitting the back of my neck. Its heat sends a shiver across my skin, a thousand goosebumps rising as my body reacts the same way it did on our first date.

He points out the window, still eyeing our group of friends. "I see Dylan and, wait, where's Reid?"

"He had to work. In fact, he took Dylan's shifts so she could come." My eyes scan the crowd, looking for the other person who I knew would be with them. "There. Her date is Riley."

Turning back around to face Spencer, I let my body fall against his, melting against his chest and laying my head on his shoulder. The smell of fresh linen, mixed with thyme and sandalwood hits my senses, acting as an aphrodisiac.

Placing a hand on each side of Spencer's face, I pull him to me and gently kiss him. At first, I softly graze my lips across his, and caress the back of his head. My fingers twist in his hair as I press his mouth more intensely and he growls, spurning me on. I'm lost in this moment, allowing myself to enjoy this man who has won my heart. And then some.

A tap on the window snaps us out of our reverie. Untangling ourselves, Spencer smooths his hair, a wicked grin playing on his lips.

He leans in for one last lingering kiss and pulls away, gripping the door handle as he readies himself for his exit. "What was that for?"

Now it's my turn. My turn to have the wicked grin. My turn to infuse the situation with a little fun, a sprinkle of surprise, and to put an extra spring into this man's step. Did I want to tell him this earlier? One hundred percent, but when I found out my news, he was already at a press junket. I had to rush to meet him at his agent's house so we could meet the car taking us to the premiere. It wasn't until we were in the car, on our way here, that we were alone.

All alone, except for the driver, but eh? He can hear the news too. Why not?

"Well," I watch over Spencer's shoulder, seeing the familiar face of one of his PR team waving at us to get out now. "I hope you're ready for your next role, Spencer."

"What do you mean? " He laughs, tugging on my hand. "C'mon we have to go now."

"Wait." I can't hold my secret any longer. "I'm pregnant."

The thrill that runs through me as I share this news with him is heady. In this one second, I know it's him and always has been. That we've gotten through what we went through because we're supposed to be us, always and forever, but we had to go through a test first. Now it's going to be three. Well, four, really, because Barney is our first baby...but you get my drift.

"Oh, my...Amelia!" His eyes crinkle at the corners as his expression changes from shock to excitement to love, and then to pure joy. He grabs me, slanting his lips across mine at the same moment that his publicist throws the back door wide open.

Talk about a good PR opportunity. If there was a contest, we'd be winning right now.

The publicist ducks her head inside the car, her eyes bouncing from Spencer to me and back again. "Okay, glad you two have each other to hold on to. It's bonkers out here tonight...you sure you two are ready for this?"

I don't need to answer, because Spencer is already out the door and holding his hand out for mine.

"You bet we are."

Thank you so much for reading The Art of Falling in Love with the Movie Star (again)!

It's Riley's turn next with **The Art of Falling in Love with Your Brother's Best Friend**! You can preorder it here if you so desire. A little hint about this one: it's going to be a brother's best friend/ice hockey romance and I cannot wait!

If you want to stay up to date on this release (and other ones too!), you can do it by signing up for my newsletter here.

If you're looking for more content like *bonus scenes, surprise chapters,* and *swag,* or maybe you want to have **early access** to Amelia and Spencer's book BEFORE it's released, then come and join me on Ream! It's a subscription service, like Netflix but waaaay more affordable and interactive, where I can give you even more stories **and** you get voting power on some of my covers, characters for books, and so much more!

Happy reading!

Anne xo

VIP Acknowledgment

THANK YOU
to
Katie Pritchett

Katie won a contest on TikTok and had naming rights for one
of the locations in this book: ***Sunflower Falls***.

Thank you so much for being such an
amazing supporter.
You're the bestest!!

To the members of the first annual Sweetkiss Creek Typo Scavenger Hunt, you know who you are, THANK YOU! I hope you had as much fun as I did. :)

To my ARC team - you're the real heroes here. You show up to read and then follow through with reviews and sharing the word. Thank you for always being so supportive. It's your energy that keeps me going!

To the person who has never been an RV before: DM me before you get one. LOL I can walk you through the pros and cons... ;)

This book is based loosely on an adventure my husband and I had in 2019/2020 in the RV we had at the time. The difference is we were traveling the South Island of New Zealand, with our terrier George Clooney, and we somehow planned a trip that took us to 18 locations in 21 days.

I. Do. Not. Condone. This. HAHAHAHA

Seriously, we saw some amazing things. The beauty of an RV is that is is just the people who are in it traveling together and you have time to really talk, but you also have to be a team to get where you want to go.

Did we fight? You bet we did. I'm a city girl, who grew up in the country, but I've always loved concrete and big build-ings. It was new to me and WOW was there a learning curve.

Did we figure things out in the end? You bet we did. In fact, we both still point to that three weeks to this day because it brought us closer together.

I'm glad we did it. We don't have the RV any longer, but

we plan on getting a caravan at some point to get back out there. I really miss being able to just go when we want and the freedom in pulling up in places that no one else has gone before is...honestly, I have no words. It blew me away.

Here's to my husband for putting up with my high-anxiety, and most of all here's to me for getting through it ;)

And here's to you...thank you for reading my book!

Anne xoxo

Here's to the Sweetheart Society!

There's this other place online where I hang out with my community, it's called Ream.

It's an online subscription platform where I drop extra behind the scenes info about Sweetkiss Creek and its residents, and play with ideas for my next books. My characters like to keep talking to me, so they needed an outlet...this is it!

I'm super lucky to have some epic folks on ream that I get to hang out with. A few of the 'locals' in the group I want to thank are:

Dana Greco, Leau Macy, and Jennifer Yeun!

These three have been hanging out with me and the others in the Sweetheart Society, getting to know Amelia and getting sneak peeks of how she and Spencer came to be. They were the first to see the book cover, and they'll be the first to see the next one too!

Want to join them and get the inside scoop as it happens, hang out with some of your favourite Sweetkiss Creek characters, or see what I'm working on next?

Join us here!

About the Author

Anne Kemp is an author of romantic comedies, sweet contemporary romance, and chick lit.
She loves reading (and does it ridiculously fast, too!), gluten-free baking
(because everyone needs a hobby that makes them crazy), and finding time to binge-watch her favorite shows. She grew up in Maryland but made Los Angeles her home until she encountered her own real-life meet-cute at a friend's wedding where she ended up married to one of the groomsmen.
For real.

Anne now lives on the Kapiti Coast in New Zealand, and even though she was married at Mt. Doom, no...she doesn't have a Hobbit. However, she and her husband do have a terrier named George Clooney and a rescue pup named Charlie. When she's not writing, she's usually with them taking a long walk on the river by their home.

www.annekemp.com

June '24

Love in Lake Lorelei Series

Ahhh...Lake Lorelei, the small town down the road from Sweetkiss Creek. These sweet romcoms are sizzling with chemistry and bringing you all the feels.

Get to know this small town, its locals and, most importantly, the Lake Lorelei Fire Department!

Sweet Summer Nights (Book 1)

Freya and Wyatt's story

The Sweet Spot (Book 2)

Ari and Carter's story

When Sparks Fly (Book 3)

Maisey and Jack's story

The Abby George Series

The Abby George books are closed-door, Chick lit comedies with a lil' sass, a touch of sarcasm, and some innuendo and language (especially from the salty captain!) but guaranteed to have you laughing out loud as you fall in love!

Rum Punch Regrets

Gotta Go To Come Back

Sugar City Secrets

Caribbean Romance Novella

Part of the Abby George world but can be read as a stand alone story.

This book is a sweet and clean closed door

romantic comedy.

Second Chance for Christmas

Stay up-to-date on new releases, get special bonus content, and special promotions when you sign up for

Anne's newsletter.

9 780047 369889